Dedication

For my dearest Rose, Tom and Joe
and my six fabulous grandchildren.

And for my seventh grandchild, Sammy Joe.

Deb Mawson

Ogo Pogo
and the
Magic Box

Written and illustrated by

Deb Mawson

Print production by
Gipping Press Ltd: Unit 2, Lion Barn Estate,
Needham Market, Suffolk, IP6 8NZ
Tel: 01449 721599
www.gippingpress.co.uk

Acknowledgements

With thanks to Catherine Legg aka 'Pernickety Kate' for her accurate and painstaking editing.

With thanks to everyone at Gipping Press for being so enthusiastic!

Chapter 1

One day an enormous rectangular cardboard box was delivered to the family home at Parham.

'What the...!?' exclaimed Alex.

'High chairs for the island,' his father, Jon, replied, in a matter-of-fact sort of voice.

'What? D'you mean Peter Pan's island, Daddy?' joked Alex.

'Oh Alex, really!' his sister Sophia giggled.

'No, don't be daft, Alex,' said Jon. 'They're for our kitchen island and we'll sit on them and eat breakfast. They're our new breakfast bar stools.'

But Alex had already disappeared, dashing upstairs like a whirlwind, returning with one of his favourite tools — his special box-opening knife.

Apart from the Guinness Book of Records, his guitars and his two goldfish aptly named Plectrum and Capo, 9½-year-old Alex's other favourite thing was his tool box. He had nearly a full range of essential tools and gadgets in his bedroom which were his pride and joy.

Alex proudly presented his father with his brand-new box-opening knife. Jon, Alex and Sophia set to it. It was quite a palaver opening that box; they all heaved, pulled, pushed, and panted heavily as Jon held the box upside down. Sophia and Alex tugged hard at its contents from underneath. Sophia went bright red with the effort, got terrible giggles and collapsed on the floor. But at last the chairs emerged and Daddy Jon unwrapped all the dreadful plastic packaging around them.

These were copper-coloured metal high stools. Very high indeed. The children's mother, Rose, came down into the kitchen at that point. She had heard all the carry on from her study. Rose worked very hard in her little room writing essays, doing research and exams in order to qualify to tell people what they should and should not eat. She was very often beavering away upstairs, but the hullabaloo brought her down.

Rose eyed the high chairs sceptically. 'They're certainly HIGH chairs, Jon,' she said.

'They're for the island, Mummy, but not Peter Pan's island or any other island on the Meare for that matter!' laughed Sophia.

'Yes, I can see that,' replied Rose drily. 'Quite high for some of us to get our thighs under the island, Jon?' She looked unimpressed and gave a little sniff.

Momentarily, Alex wondered if he should dash upstairs and get his small saw. He thought he could suggest cutting one of the stool's legs shorter so Mummy could fit more easily under the island.

By now Sophia had totally lost interest in the chairs and was eyeing up the empty box.

'Look at the size of it!' exclaimed Sophia. 'It's taller than me... It's taller than you, Alex! It's huge!'

'It's great!' agreed Alex excitedly.

'Daddy, can we have this box to play in?' asked Sophia.

But before Daddy could reply, the two children had turned it on its side and were crawling inside.

'WOW! It's dark in here! Wow, it's amazing! There's room for both of us – come on!' Sophia said. They started trying to roll it over and over as they wriggled inside it.

At that point, Tinkerbell, the family's beautiful — but nervous — tortoiseshell cat, emerged into the kitchen from her cosy, safe, curled up sleeping position on Sophia's bed. This was next to Sophia's life-sized stuffed tiger called 'Sneakers'. All cats together. Suddenly Tinkerbell was hissing and spitting, all her hair sticking out like a hedgehog. The box seemed to be rolling itself all over the kitchen floor with a lot of muffled shrieks coming from inside.

'Oh dear,' muttered Rose, who could see a catastrophe occurring. 'Now just a minute you two, this kitchen is not a playroom and you need to take that box somewhere else. Take it out up to the den.'

Some chanting came from inside the box as the children sang:

'We play in the box,
We play in the box,
We play in the box,
All day!'

'Right! That's enough! Out now, you two!'

So the children reluctantly wriggled out and lugged the huge container to the back door. Tinkerbell scarpered quickly ahead of them, away across the garden, as the children pulled the box across the path and up the outside stairs of the garage.

The room above the garage was their den that Jon had so cleverly built over the car port. Jon was always building things. Having been practically born with a spanner in his hand, Alex had learned nearly everything he knew about tools and stuff about building from his father. In fact, Jon and Rose had built the entire house they lived in 10 years earlier, and were real geniuses at doing projects around it nowadays.

But as far as the children were concerned, the den was the epitome of genius. Inside it had a floor large enough for roller skating, a table tennis table, table football, disco lights, a smoke machine and a sound system. Alex and Sophia loved it and so did their cousins and friends.

'Righto! In here!' they cried.

'We play in the box,
We play in the box,
We play in the box,
All day!'

They adored it. They could both stand up in it, lie in it, shuffle about in it and generally fall about laughing in it. It was totally brilliant, and even better, it was SO sturdy, it did not fall apart, it did not collapse and it took quite a hammering and still looked new.

'Wow! It's just SO strong!' exclaimed Sophia. 'It's amazing — it never looks battered or any older. It must be very well made indeed!' She wriggled out and inspected all the corners and sides. 'They just haven't changed and they're not at all dirty either! Isn't that clever?'

'A bit weird if you ask me,' replied Alex. 'Let's try a bit harder to make it collapse.'

So, giggling, they wriggled and twisted, thumped the sides from inside, both leaned on one side together, got out and jumped on it, but with everything they did, the box just kept springing back into shape and continued looking brand new.

'SUPPER TIME!' they heard their mother's voice calling from the back door. They knew better than not to come when called. Besides which, Rose's food was always so delicious — and they were starving.

'Come on!' said Sophia 'Let's leave it for now — but it does seem that there is something just a little bit unusual about this box!'

'Definitely,' replied Alex as they left it lying on its side.

And with that they closed the door of the room and clattered down the stairs.

But had they, just for a moment, glanced back to the box, they might have seen a tiny pair of very bright green eyes winking and blinking at them from the dark interior of it.

Chapter 2

Luckily for everyone, the next day was Saturday. The children's best morning was Saturday. Mainly because they were allowed to watch some TV for an hour.

The children raced downstairs with their duvets to get the TV on at precisely 7am. 'Good-oh! It's our favourite — Shaun the Sheep!' they chimed as they got stuck in. Snuggling under their duvets, they sucked their thumbs, gawping at the screen.

After a bit it was time for breakfast.

'Now then,' said Rose, 'Daddy's going to take care of you this morning while I go out and do some work to catch up. I'll be back at lunchtime and we'll go on an exciting outing, I promise! And later, your cousins are coming over for tea so perhaps we'll make a camp fire in the woods,' she added. Rose had a very adventurous nature and she often created magical outward-bound challenges with the children.

'Yes, children,' said Jon, 'I've got a few jobs to do around the garage, so can you play outside or in the den for an hour or so?'

Sophia and Alex eyed each other up. This was music to their ears. There was nothing they liked more than messing about together.

As soon as they had slurped back their smoothies and gobbled up their delicious Saturday green waffles, they put on their jackets and trainers and ran outside. It was a beautiful early summer's day. The sort that makes you feel good to be alive. The birds were singing — the day felt really great and full of promise. Sophia was excited!

'What shall we do?' said Alex, who was looking forward to time with his toys after his busy week at school. He had it in mind that he wanted to experiment with his bicycle multi-functional-horn/bell-and-excellent-rude-noise-handlebar accessory, which his best friend had given him for his 9th birthday a few months earlier.

'What?!' exclaimed Sophia. 'I know exactly what we're going to do! We're heading to the den to get on with our box game. OK, Alex?'

'Oh OK,' he replied a little unenthusiastically. He was thinking about his tool kit, and his bike multi-functional gadget again. Or he would have liked them to do something creative, like build a rocket machine to send into space, or cut up some of his bungee collection with his Stanley knife to make a zip wire.

'Come on Alex, it'll be great fun!' And she hauled him up the side stairs of the garage.

Sophia was always full of vigour. There was no end to it. She could run, skip, do cartwheels and handstands, play netball, do ballet, go to brownies and running club all in a day and would still be full of sparkle at the end of it. Although 19 months younger than Alex, at the age of nearly 8 she was as tall as Alex and had just as much energy as him. She was definitely here for living life to the full, always ready to do something exciting.

Sophia's favourite expression was 'Oh my God!' which she had learnt from her cheeky Uncle Tom, her mother's brother. He was always saying it, and she loved saying it too. Only Sophia's mother Rose wasn't too keen on it being used and so Sophia usually said it out of earshot unless she wanted to wind her Mummy up, which she often did with great ease.

Sophia's other great love, apart from reading, was all things to do with animals. She adored them and was truly kind and good with all animals. Her bedroom was full of her named toy animal creatures — Tinkerbell, the family cat, loved it in there. But Sophia was particularly fond of Bunty. Sophia's Mummy's mother, called Gar Gar, had a black and white Springador — a naughty, enthusiastic dog — and Sophia was proud to think that she was the only grandchild who could actually make Bunty do as she was told, most of the time, anyway. Sophia's cousin, Harry, also doted on Bunty because he spent time with her when he was a toddler. But Sophia was a force to be reckoned with as far as Bunty was concerned.

As they swung the door wide open and came into the room, Sophia stopped dead in her tracks.

'What the...? Alex, are you thinking what I'm thinking? That box was lying on its side last night and now it's... well... upright!'

'P'raps Mummy moved it or Daddy picked it up?' suggested Alex.

'Oh yes, maybe... let's ask Daddy.' They hollered down the stairs at Jon, but he called back that he hadn't touched it.

'Never mind, it must have been Mummy... let's get inside,' said Sophia.

So they set it up right again and this time they managed to get inside with the box the right way up. It involved standing on the sofa and jumping, one at a time, into it. They started laughing immediately. There was something so funny about it.

'Ooh, it's so dark, ooh, it's so big I can hardly see the top anymore! The box seems to be getting deeper and deeper!' exclaimed Sophia.

And they started chanting again:

'We play in the box,
We play in the box,
We play in the box,
All day!'

But then something absolutely ridiculous happened. The box started moving, not from their wriggling, not from their swaying, but of its OWN accord. They could feel it shudder and vibrate. They felt it moving, a bit like being in a lift, but lurching sideways and they realised it had taken off the floor and was airborne. It felt smooth and quiet, but no matter how hard they looked, the top of the box was out of reach and there was nothing to see except some dim light.

Without them realising it, the box had in fact taken flight and was now moving spontaneously towards the open door.

'Whoa! Wait a minute! Stop!' they shouted. 'Daddy! Help!' they screamed (and Sophia had a very loud voice, but even so, Daddy did not reply)... but nothing stopped the box flying through the door and the children realised they could not be heard.

On the box flew, upwards and outwards with the two children inside it. They were slightly scared, but at the same time it was all really curious and this felt pretty magical.

'Perhaps this is a dream. I think we should just sit down and wait and see what happens,' said Alex. 'After all it's bound to come down somewhere.' They sat down cross-legged either side of the bottom of the box. By now the sunlight from the top had created a rather nice golden glow inside.

'I say, Alex, supposing someone sees this box flying about... they'd think it was pretty strange,' giggled Sophia.

'I hope it doesn't decide to do a somersault or a back flip,' he laughed, although he was actually feeling rather nervous.

They sat there for a little while longer.

Suddenly Sophia gave a yelp. 'OUCH! I seem to be sitting on something!' She felt around her backside and there in the corner she found a matchbox — just an ordinary-looking matchbox.

Sophia shook the match box but it did not rattle like match boxes normally did. Instead, she heard the tiniest, high pitched little squeal.

Gingerly, Sophia slid open the match box. 'Oh my God!' she breathed.

Chapter 3

A tiny elderly creature was blinking at her from inside the matchbox. He had a little head with a whirl of rather long white hair, a little pixie hat, tiny upturned nose and bright green eyes the colour of the sea. Wearing a little mustard-coloured sleeveless jerkin and a pair of dark green leggings, he had a small body and skinny little arms and legs. On his feet he wore battered old shoes. He seemed to the children to look ancient. He was about the size of Sophia's little finger.

The little creature looked rather bad tempered. 'Do you mind?' it squawked. 'You nearly squashed me!'

'I'm terribly sorry,' whispered Sophia soothingly, who, as we know, could be charming with little animals. 'I didn't know you were there, or else I would never have sat on you.'

'I think... I think... I know who he is,' said Alex slowly to Sophia. 'He's Mummy's childhood friend Ogo Pogo!'

'NO I'M NOT!' squeaked the little creature grumpily. 'I'm Ogo Pogo's brother — Ege Pege. And don't discuss me with your sister as if I'm not in the room. That's very rude.'

'Sorry!' Alex felt put in his place. Ogo Pogo and Ege Pege (pronounced Ohgo Pohgo and Eegee Peegee) were two little characters who came to live at Rose cottage when Alex and Sophia's mummy, Rose, and her two brothers, Tom and Joe, were children. Grandpa Anthony had introduced his three children to these tiny characters and they had had many extraordinary adventures together. Anthony had also told many stories about the two little brothers and what they got up to while Rose, Tom and Joe were at school. Rose was very keen on these stories, very fond of the Ogo Pogo and Ege Pege, and remembered exactly the antics of her childhood friends.

Ogo Pogo and Ege Pege now lived in a matchbox on the windowsill in Alex's room at their house in Parham. Rose often related stories about them to Alex and Sophia. Recently, the two naughty little brothers had got into a lot of trouble sneaking into Alex and Sophia's very own school bags and turning up at school. Then there had also been the near disaster at the pond with Ogo and Ege nearly drowning the kittens Luna and Marmalade. But Alex and Sophia had never before actually SEEN them (or the kittens). When they looked in the matchbox they were never there, but the children knew instinctively that this was one of them in real life, at last.

'Crikey!' said Alex, 'I never actually believed in them… did you, Soph?'

'DO YOU MIND! I HEARD THAT,' squawked the little fellow crossly. 'Now look here you two. I don't mind telling you that I'm very upset today and I'd like a little consideration, please.'

'We're terribly sorry, Ege Pege— please accept our apologies,' replied Sophia respectfully (she really was amazing at managing small creatures), as she held the matchbox very gently in her outstretched palm.

'But, well, we feel a bit surprised and very confused by everything that's going on, that's all. We've never been in a flying cardboard box before and we don't quite know why we're here.' (At that she nearly started giggling again at the absurdity of it all.) 'Also, we weren't expecting actually to see you. By the way... how do you do, Ege Pege? It's very nice to meet you at last. I'm Sophia and this is Alex.'

'Yes, yes of course, I know exactly who you are,' he replied irritably. And less rudely he added, 'I don't mean to sound so grumpy, but I'm in a bit of a pickle, very upset, and I desperately need your help.'

'Right well, of course we'll do whatever we can to help you. You must tell us exactly what the problem is,' replied Alex solemnly. But he actually thought *It's a true fact that we're ALL in a pickle and I'm not sure what we're supposed to do from inside this blinking box, with no tools.*

'Well, the main problem,' squeaked Ege Pege, 'is that I've lost my brother Ogo Pogo. It's a disaster!' And then Ege began to cry.

"Do you mind? I heard that"
squawked the little fellow crossly.

Chapter 4

It was a very high pitched and tiny crying noise (not a bit like Sophia's, for instance), and he shed actual wet tears and the children felt very sorry for him. The matchbox started filling up, like a little bath.

'Oh, please stop crying Ege,' said Alex. 'You're going to get dreadfully wet — you'll end up sitting in a matchbox of tear water and that won't help Ogo at all. Now please tell us exactly what happened and then we can make a proper assessment of the situation.' He was privately thinking about the Health and Safety aspects of this predicament. He had noticed that his Daddy used that expression and agreed that it was probably important to think about those things in most situations. Sitting in a flying cardboard box, going to who knows where, did not strike him as very safe at all.

Ege Pege continued in his squeaky voice in between sniffs. 'Well, yesterday, while you and Sophia were at school, Ogo and I were flying your super red Lego aeroplane in your bedroom, Alex. We were having a great time seeing who could be launched into the air the highest. We took it in turns to sit in the cockpit. Rose had opened the window to air the bedroom while you were out. One time, we did such an amazing launch that the plane shot out of the window and into the garden with Ogo Pogo sitting inside the pilot's seat.'

Ege Pege sniffed hard at the memory. 'Ogo was shouting and waving and yelling something to me, but I couldn't exactly hear what he was saying. And the next thing I knew, he had disappeared over the top of the trees and was out of view. And the terrible thing is that he hasn't come back.' At that Ege really started sobbing.

One time we did such an amazing launch
that the plane shot out of the window and into the garden
with Ogo Pogo sitting in the pilot's seat

In between sobs he added, squeakily, 'Now, our matchbox doesn't really have much magic power and I couldn't follow him very far (*sniff*). It can go little distances, but not miles and miles. Anyway, even if I could, the matchbox wouldn't have enough power to fly back with two of us in it. Really, because the matchbox is so ancient, it needs re-boosting often to go anywhere. And the worst thing of all, is that I don't know where Ogo's gone.' Ege started welling up again and copious amounts of water sprouted from his eyes.

'Oh dear, that really is terrible. But what are WE doing in this box?' enquired Alex sensibly. 'What have WE got to do with it all?'

'You're the key to finding Ogo,' replied Ege.

'What do you mean?' asked Alex suspiciously. 'How can we find him, when we're stuck in here?'

'Well, you got the box moving and flying with your magic spell,' replied Ege.

'What the...?' both the children exclaimed at once.

'Yes,' said Ege with a sigh. 'You see, you chanted the magic spell that made the box fly and all I have to do now is add the words to help the box know where to go, except I don't know what to say... and now I'm running out of time.'

'Please explain, Ege, I'm completely baffled,' said Sophia.

'Me too!' said Alex. 'What magic spell did we use — and when?' he continued.

'Well, you sang it really... It went like this:
We play in the box,

We play in the box,
We play in the box,
All day!'

'WHAT! That's a magic spell? It can't be! It's just a normal set of words, nothing clever — no hocus pocus, abracadabra, or anything magic about THOSE words,' said Alex.

'Yes, but there is,' squeaked Ege. 'You see, you both chanted them identically at the same time together, and when I heard you, I realised all I had to do was to say the words too to add a tiny amount magic, and we'd have a proper spell on our hands. That's why the box can fly.'

Alex and Sophia looked at each other with amazement.

'This is really spooky, Ege Pege. So what do you want us to do now? We'll do what we can to help. But firstly, please explain why you are running out of time,' added Alex.

'Well,' squeaked Ege, 'I can only go so far from home in this matchbox and shortly I will need to get back to the window sill to recharge its batteries – so to speak. The sunlight gives the matchbox enough power to get us a little way from home. And it's OK while we are currently hovering over the top of the pond. If we go any further from the house, I will lose all my energy.'

'*Yikes!*' thought Alex as he imagined the big box dive bombing into it, from a great height, and making an enormous splash with all of them in it.

'But how do you know we're over the pond, Ege?' asked Sophia. 'I can't see out of the top — it's too high up.'

'If you look carefully in this corner of the box behind where you were sitting, there is a tiny hole. And Alex, put this little straw through the hole like this, and then look through the top of the straw with your eye. Now you can see everything that's going on underneath the box.'

'Well, I never saw that,' said Alex with curiosity. 'Let's try!' And sure enough, he could see everything that was going on below. 'Wow that really is magic!' Sophia had a look too and was beginning to wonder where this was all leading.

'So,' said Ege, 'I'm going to have leave you soon and get home, but I'm entrusting you both with the task of finding Ogo Pogo, otherwise it will be a disaster for everyone, especially your Mummy. All you will have to do is to keep flying, telling the box where to go, and keep looking. If you land, you must use the magic spell to get the box flying. Make sure you chant the spell exactly at the same time...'

Alex inwardly groaned as he considered the distress it would cause his mother to find that Ogo had gone permanently missing.

'Hold on a minute! Wait!' shouted Sophia. 'I've got another question; you said you couldn't 'exactly' hear what Ogo was yelling... Did you hear ANY of it – anything at all?'

'Er, yes...' muttered Ege, 'but it makes no sense at all. I could only just hear what he said, and I may be wrong as it was very faint. But what I heard... was the word JOE!'

With that, Ege Pege jumped into his matchbox and slid it shut, and before they could stop him, it shot up into the sky, through the top of the open box, and disappeared from view.

"Yikes!" thought Alex as he imagined the big box dive bombing in the pond with all of them in it!

Chapter 5

Alex and Sophia looked at each other in dismay.

'Now what are we supposed to do?' Sophia said gloomily, 'I know we MUST help Ege and Ogo, but I really can't think where we should start looking.'

'Yes, and I'm getting very hungry,' replied Alex.

Suddenly Sophia had a brainwave. 'Alex... do you think the word 'JOE' has anything to do with Uncle Joe? You know, Mummy said that when he was a little boy, Joe her youngest brother used to do magic tricks. In fact, he was known as "Magic Joe". Gar Gar told me that he was very good at them. He used to do magic shows and stuff, charging the rest of the family to come and see his shows. He might be able to help us to decide where to look for Ogo or he might have a clue or be able to use some magic spells to help us.'

'Soph - you're an absolute genius — for two reasons. Firstly, for remembering that uncle Joe used to be called "Magic Joe" when he was a little boy, and secondly because Auntie Clare makes the best sandwiches ever!'

'Right ho! Let's go!' And together they chanted the magic words. At the end Alex added, — 'Take us to Uncle Joe's house!' As soon as they spoke the words, the box veered off to the south and west and whooshed over the tree tops and houses towards Ipswich.

Suddenly Alex gave a shout. 'Wait! STOP!'

The box stopped in its tracks immediately and came to a hovering halt.

'Oh, ALEX — for goodness' sake! What ARE YOU DOING! Why did you say "stop" like that?! I've been thrown over to the other side of the box and nearly got that straw stuck in my ear!' yelled Sophia, infuriated.

'Well, sorry Soph, but I had an idea and I needed the box to stop. I just had a thought… Oy, budge over and let me look down that straw. Yes… I thought so, we're virtually going over Kettleburgh.'

'SO WHAT?' shouted Sophia, still very annoyed.

'Well, Soph, Uncle Tom lives here, doesn't he? Look, that's their house. And we know for a true fact that the family are back from Germany this weekend as they're all supposed to be coming for tea today.'

'Well, who knows where we'll be at tea time,' Sophia muttered under her breath.

'Now look here, Sophia — we've got to do ALL we can to find Ogo. Uncle Tom knows quite a bit about Ogo and Ege because they were part of Tom's childhood too, and I think we should talk to him. Uncle Tom might have some ideas about where he might be heading. And we should call in here on the way to Joe's.'

'But Alex, we can't just turn up, like this, in a flying box,' Sophia pointed out peevishly.

'Hmmm,' said Alex 'I suppose we could drop down the other side of their hedge and walk in through the gate, casually, and then gradually try and bring the topic of conversation round to Ogo Pogo and Ege Pege.'

Sophia thought for a couple of minutes. She was staring at the ground. Finally, and with more enthusiasm, she turned to her brother and said, 'Look, Alex. We haven't got much time and we need to get on with it. I really think we have to show Uncle Tom the box and tell him everything about it. I suggest we land it in the drive way and just get out as quickly as possible.'

So that's what they did. They landed in the driveway. Climbed out, put the box upright and went to knock on the side door. There was a lot of barking and meowing coming from inside. But the door didn't open. But quite soon a rather damp looking Uncle Tom walked around the corner of the house holding a hose in his hand.

'I say! Hello, you two, what a great surprise! How lovely to see you on this beautiful morning. Scuse me looking a bit wet and muddy, I was just cleaning up the ride-on. The girls are playing dogs and cats inside — you can probably hear them. They'll be so pleased to see you! How are you, Sophia and Alex? How the dickens did you get here...? Did Mummy drop you off or did you cycle, or...?' And then he caught sight of the box in the drive, while at the same time, Sophia launched herself at Tom, and jumping up into his arms gave him the most enormous hug. Sophia adored Tom, who was also her Godfather.

At Tom's House (by Sophia)

Tom opened the door wide and Beatrix and Bella came charging, and flung themselves at Alex and Sophia. They loved their cousins. Alex could make Bella laugh till she was nearly sick, and Bea had wonderful friendships with both Alex and Sophia. Bea and Sophia often had the best fun times anyone can ever imagine. They both loved drawing and playing at anything to do with animals. Bea, bright as a button, with a great sense of humour, thoughtful, sensible and kind, had the thickest golden hair you've ever seen. She was only 6 months younger than Sophia.

Bella, nearly 5, was sturdy and quick witted, with lovely curly hair cut in a bob. She was self-contained, determined, and definitely able to hold her own in the crowd. She adored playing endlessly with her vast selection of Sylvania family toys, her model horses, and a toy cat who could eat, meow and purr. Purrfect!

'Wow!' they cried. Then Bea continued, 'What are you two doing here? We thought we were coming to tea with you later. Mummy's just cycled into town to get the ingredients for us all to make a cake to bring to your house. We're going to make one of Mummy's delicious luscious lemon cakes. But so great to see you! We're just playing dogs and cats... come and join us!'

'No wait!' said Alex seriously. 'I'm sorry Bea — we would love to otherwise, but there's something very urgent that we must discuss with you, Uncle Tom. We don't have very long I'm afraid.'

'Right, well, you'd better come straight inside.' And he gestured them into the dining room to sit at the table. 'Have a glass of cold water and here... um ... here are some cashew nuts of Auntie Dee Dee's and tell me all about it.' Uncle Tom sat them down with some ice-cubed water and a bowl of nuts which Alex devoured with great animation. They all sat round the table and all eyes looked at Alex and Sophia.

And so the story began. Alex started it but Sophia got it going along nicely, because she is a really good and quick speaker. Alex and Sophia told them the whole story about Ogo Pogo being launched in Alex's red Lego aeroplane and all the rest. It was quite a lot to tell and they were pretty exhausted by the end. Tom had not interrupted once and had listened very attentively. 'So that's why we're here, Uncle Tom, and we wondered if you had any ideas or advice,' she concluded.

Tom was holding his gin and tonic very carefully and then slowly placed it down on the table. He looked at them with his steady grey eyes and said very firmly and seriously, 'Oh my God, children, this is a terrible situation. You must do WHATEVER it takes to find Ogo Pogo. It would be an absolute disaster if he got lost. Rose would never forgive you or any of us, and she would be very, very unhappy for a very long time, as indeed would Joe and I. He is smaller than my little finger, and all manner of dangers are lurking out there for a little chap like him. He could be eaten in one mouthful by a naughty dog like Bunty for instance.' Everyone suddenly shivered at the image of Bunty eating Ogo Pogo.

'My suggestion is that you get straight back in that box and go directly over to see Uncle Joe in Nacton. I think he might have more ideas than me. However, I have got two things to say, though. One is that Ogo Pogo always wanted to fly in an aeroplane. When I was a boy of your age, Alex, I once found him trying to take off in one of my Airfix model fighter jets and he was most put out when he realised it was glued to the stand.' (Bea and Sophia started giggling when Tom said that).'Ogo told me in that squeaky voice of his that one day he fully intended to find an aeroplane to fly to visit his cousins in New Zealand. And I'm a bit worried that he thinks now is the time to do it.'

'But Daddy! That's miles away! That's further away than Germany! Why it's right round the other side of the world!' exclaimed Bea. 'It would take him days and days to get there, especially on Alex's model Lego aeroplane, it would be crazy! Anything could happen to him on the way'. Everybody looked at her and nodded vigorously. 'That's a true fact, Bea,' said Alex.

'Well, I could be wrong,' admitted Tom, 'but he certainly had a desire to fly in an aeroplane and perhaps this has been his only real chance.'

'And what's the second thing, Tom?' asked Alex gravely.

'Well, it's just a hunch I have, but I wonder if that big flying box does not use up earthly time, as we know it, when it flies. Travel machines often have strange time clocks. What I mean is, that no matter how long you travel in it, you might arrive back at your starting point at around the same time that you left it. You might take up time in it and out of it, and need food and sleep and rest, but I believe when you get back to home it could be just about the same moment as when you left.'

'WOW! That's cool,' said all three girls simultaneously.

'OK, Alex and Sophia, let's do an experiment to test my hunch. Here's what I want you to do. I want you to get into the box, set your watch and fly round the house for precisely five minutes and then land back on the drive. Can you do that?'

So, remembering to say the magic chant first, Alex and Sophia took off and flew round the house for exactly five minutes. The box disappeared from view several times.

When they landed back, Tom exclaimed, 'Yep! Thought so. You have only been gone exactly 10 seconds by my stop watch. That will be 120 seconds per hour (2 minutes) and so that would be about 48 minutes even if you were gone for a full 24 hours, which is very unlikely indeed.'

Alex made the additions in his head and looked suitably impressed.

'Wow!' said Sophia, 'that's just what happened in a book I read. I never thought it could happen to us, not in real life.'

'Right now, this makes life much easier. I don't need to say anything to Auntie Dee Dee at the moment, because you will be going forwards in time, but you will hardly be gone for any time at all. Likewise, Rose needn't know anything about it at this stage. Right, so in you get. Yes, ALL of you, in you go!'

Bea didn't have to be invited twice. Bella was a little more hesitant. They were both amazed to be allowed to go on such a dangerous and important mission.

'But Daddy, aren't you just the teeniest bit worried about us — about us being safe?' asked Bella who was unsure about getting in that box. 'I mean, what will Mummy say? And really, I don't know if I want to go!'

'Nonsense, I'm not in the slightest bit worried,' replied Tom. 'You'll be back before we know it and I believe it's of the utmost importance that we get this box going as quickly as we can. Mummy would agree, I'm sure, and we need ALL your voices together saying the magic spell to make it travel as fast as it can go. And we need ALL your brains to think hard where to go! And we need Joe!' Holding the box on its side he said in a loud voice, 'Now crawl in and off you go!'

And as they did a strange thing happened. The box appeared to expand in size so that it didn't feel doubly cramped with four of them in it, it just seemed the same. They sat in the corners of the box and chorused the magic chant:

'We play in the box,
We play in the box,
We play in the box,

All day!'
Take us to Uncle Joe's house.'

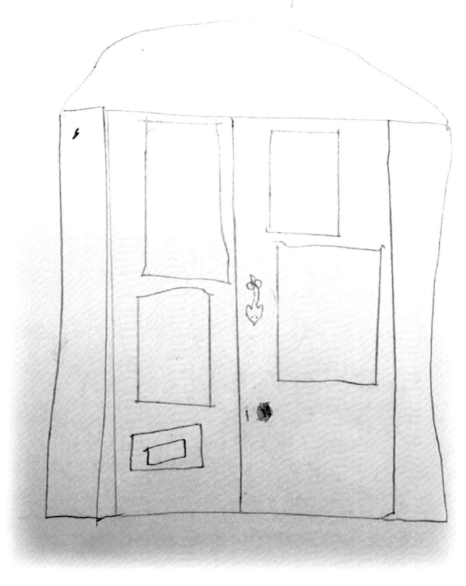

They knocked loudly with the brass dolphin knocker (by Harry)

Chapter 6

They flew away from the village of Kettleburgh
out towards Wickham Market and over the A12
heading south. Alex was taking charge and kept
checking their progress through the straw and
reporting back to the others. The tree tops looked
beautifully green and fresh on that sunny morning.

The sky was blue and the sunlight cast a warm
glow inside the box. The others kept complaining
that they wanted to see through the straw as well.
But in the end they gave up because it would be
so confusing to keep changing places.

To keep everyone calm, Alex and Sophia
explained to their cousins Bea and Bella
everything they knew about Ogo Pogo and Ege
Pege. The sisters also added a few things of their
own that their daddy Tom had told them. 'So you
see,' Alex said, 'these two little creatures are
very special to our Mummy, your Daddy and to
Uncle Joe.'

'I did know about those two naughty boys,
because Daddy told us,' said Bella, 'and I know all
about Grandpa Anthony who is in heaven playing
cribbage, and Daddy was very sad about that.'

'Yes,' agreed Alex, 'that's what makes it all
the more important to find Ogo'.

Alex had a soft spot for Bella and was very
kind to her including her in the cousins' games.
Although she was only 4 and a half, he knew she
was a brave girl. Gar Gar was always telling Alex

that as he was her oldest grandchild, he had to take care of ALL the cousins, set a good example. He could feel the responsibility acutely right now, and was a little nervous.

Alex had another look down the straw and realised they were approaching Nacton Village and Joe's and Clare's house.

'RIGHT, we're nearly here. Soph, what do you think is the best way to go about this?'

Sophia was thinking hard for a minute. She knew Joe would be calm and kind, as he always was, but she did wonder how their cousins Harry and Ellie would react to them all arriving in this box.

'I think what we did at Uncle Tom's was the RIGHT thing to do, she said. I think we need to be HONEST and be as quick as we can.'

They landed the box in the path that runs up to the front door of their Uncle Joe and Auntie Clare's house. They wriggled out, pulled it away from any view to the road or curious passers-by. Then they boldly stepped up to the front door and knocked loudly with the brass dolphin knocker. They could hear some guitar playing coming from inside the house. Alex knew this first-rate playing was his uncle Joe's. Alex loved Uncle Joe, also his Godfather, and especially for his guitar playing. He was just so cool; Alex was always so thrilled when Joe taught him riffs and stuff on the guitar.

They knocked again.

The big heavy door opened a crack, then gradually wider and a little girl with a beaming smile looked up at them with astonishment

'Mummy! Daddy! Guess what! Guess who's here!'

'Who is it?' Called Daddy from the next room, still playing his guitar.

'Daddy! It's MY COUSINS!' shouted little Ellie who was delighted to see them. 'It's my Suffolk cousins!' she added to clarify.

Ellie was wearing her favourite spotty dog outfit and started woofing at her cousins excitedly. Bella woofed back and the two of them went off on all fours down the hallway to the kitchen.

Joe put his guitar carefully on its stand and went to the front door, half expecting Ellie to have been playing a trick on him.

'Good heavens! Hello! What are you all doing here? I was expecting to see you all at tea time at Rose and Jon's house. How did you get here? Are Tom or Rose here as well? How lovely!' Joe opened the front door wide and let the four of them all troop in while he scanned the road beyond with curiosity. Their cousin Harry was busy building the biggest Lego train track Alex had ever seen. It was running all the way down the hallway and back again.

'Hi Alex!' grinned Harry, 'Wow! Hi Sophia! Hi Bea! Hi Bella!' And he looked immensely pleased to see them all. Beaming from ear to ear with his gappy teeth, he added, 'Oh this is great, will you all come and play with me with my train set?'

Alex would have loved to, as he thought Harry's Lego trains were brilliant, and was about to, but Sophia nudged him and cleared her throat.

'We're very sorry, Harry, but we haven't come to play — we need to talk to Uncle Joe urgently and we don't have much time, do we?' She looked sternly at the others, who nodded seriously.

'Right, well then,' said Joe, 'We were about to have some sandwiches for a lunchtime picnic. Would you like some too and then you can tell us all about it?'

Clare was beyond the hallway in the kitchen preparing lunch. They could hear her singing.

'Clare! Clare! We've got visitors, could we make a few more sandwiches?'

Clare looked absolutely astonished and delighted when the four cousins walked into the kitchen. 'Well, good heavens above! How lovely to see you, but what are you doing here and more importantly how did you get here?'

'We need to talk to Uncle Joe urgently if that's ok please, and we'd absolutely love some sandwiches,' said Bea. 'Thank you, Auntie Clare,' she added politely.

'Well, of course,' smiled Clare, whose sandwiches were always just the best. 'Is it a private matter, or can you tell us all over lunch?' she asked.

'No, we can ALL talk about it', replied Bea. 'We've got something really important and urgent to do and we need all the help we can get.'

Harry muttered something about going outside to play some football with everyone — he was eyeing up the cousins and working out team sides, handicaps and positions for them all. He could see a perfect opportunity for a really exciting game of four a side. But Sophia said, 'We need you too, Harry. You're the year representative for your school committee and you know the sort of things to say in a meeting.'

'Oh alright,' said Harry bashfully, 'but perhaps we can play some football after lunch?'

'I doubt it, I'm afraid, Harry,' said Bea (who secretly found football absolutely exhausting). 'This really is super-important.'

Harry, blond, could run like the wind, was great fun, super-bright, incredibly well-read, brilliant at all board and card games (especially chess), also aged 7½ (just 3 weeks older than Bea). He began to feel that his potential family football game was in danger of being side-lined. Football, to him, WAS super-important. He was 90% serious about it and intended to become a professional footballer when he grew up. But he knew better than to make a fuss and anyway, he was starving and ready for his Mummy's sandwiches.

'Right well, come on then — what's this all about?' Uncle Joe said calmly.

So Sophia launched into the whole story yet again, with regular chippings in from the others. She did a good job, keeping to the point. When it got to the bit about the flying box, Joe, Clare and Harry's eyes seemed to grow huge like saucers and they all three felt they absolutely had to leave the table to go out to the front garden to inspect the box. Scuse us,' they said, 'we'll be back in a minute!'

They came back in stunned silence. 'Continue!' said Joe. And they carried on until it got to the end and where they were all sitting now round the kitchen table.

There was a lengthy silence as the children, munching their sandwiches, stared anxiously at Joe. It was hard to know what he was thinking Joe was looking down at the table cloth, tracing patterns on it with his forefinger. He had stopped eating. He had a faraway, concentrated look about him.

Then looking up at them, he saw the six pairs of expectant eyes looking back at him. He straightened his back, cleared his throat, took a sip of his beer and began to talk candidly.

'Alright now then. Children, this is indeed a very serious problem. Tom is right, you HAVE to go and find Ogo Pogo urgently. It would be a very sad and bad thing indeed if he got lost. Not only would Rose, Tom and I be very VERY upset, but in addition, such an event would most likely mean the end of Ege Pege.'

Chapter 7

There was a sharp intake of breath from around the table.

'Oh my God!' gasped Sophia immediately – and then seeing Joe's expression, quickly changed it to 'Oh my goodness!'

'Well,' continued Joe, 'don't you see? Those two little chaps are like Siamese twins. They are so alike, so connected, that they are practically one creature. They rely on each other totally for energy, for life, for company, for everything. If one of them were to disappear, the other would not survive long without him. In addition, they both need to be IN their matchbox for a certain amount of time every day. It's where they get their sustenance and their power from. The matchbox on the window sill recharges them. That's why Ege was so distressed and why he needed your help so badly. Now, why Ogo shouted my name is not clear,' said Joe modestly. 'You see, I think he might have meant the other 'Joe'. I'm not **THE** original 'Magic Joe'. I just used to be called 'Magic Joe' by my Mummy (your Gar Gar) and by my Daddy (your grandpa Anthony). I used to do magic tricks, yes, but I think I've probably forgotten most of it. THE 'Magic Joe' is another little creature that our father Anthony used to tell us about. He lived somewhere in the woods at Redgrave where we were brought up. But what we really don't know for sure is whether Ogo Pogo's last shout to Ege Pege was about THE Magic Joe, or about me.'

'Ooh yes, I remember you telling us about Grandpa Anthony's stories!' exclaimed Harry.

'Well, I know ALL about Grandpa Anthony actually,' interrupted Bella, 'He would be very upset in heaven, if Ogo Pogo got lost. My Daddy Tom would not like it one bit.'

'Nor me!' added Ellie, for good measure.

'True fact,' replied Alex quietly.

'But wait!' continued Harry, 'Daddy, I ACTUALLY believe you ARE THE Magic Joe. I know you are! You can often predict things that come true, you often seem able to read my mind, and Mummy's and Ellie's, you often seem to have extra understanding and you can still do magic tricks and are AMAZING at card games and chess and you know all sorts of magical as well as factual things about life and the world!'

'Well thanks, Harry!' replied Joe.

'Look, Uncle Joe, said Sophia 'we think you might be able to sort of... um...reach out... er... in your mind... so to speak... er... how do I say this?...with your mind's eye... inside your mind... sort of, and see if you get any hunches or messages as to what's going on with Ogo Pogo, where he might be and if he's still OK. Uncle Tom thought you could help, and we think you can too.'

'Yes, Uncle Joe, I've heard that's called *Extra Sensory Perspiration*,' said Alex knowingly... 'It's the sixth and extra sense, and we think you might have that ESP, and help us get an idea about Ogo Pogo's whereabouts.'

'I think you'll find that word's *'Perception'*... Extra Sensory Perception, actually,' smiled Clare, who had been listening quietly.

'Well, I don't know,' replied Joe to Alex. 'I'm not sure, I might be a bit rusty these days. But I suppose it's worth a try, but I'd need ALL your help.'

But before he could continue, Clare held up her hand as if to stop the conversation. Everyone ceased talking.

'Now look here, everyone! Excuse me for butting in, but this seems all a bit crazy. You are saying you need ALL the children to be involved in this rescue operation? I do see — I do totally understand — that it's vitally important that Ogo Pogo is found, for all of you, Joe, but I'm certainly not very happy about Ellie going anywhere in a flying box. She's only nearly 4...' Clare suddenly looked confused 'Wait a minute! Where IS Ellie? And for that matter where IS Bella?' Clare looked around the room...

Suddenly they realised that there was a lot of barking and meowing coming from upstairs. While all that serious talking had been going on, the two youngest cousins had crawled out under the table and slipped away, now happily playing cats and dogs in the bedroom.

'Actually,' said Clare, I think that's the best thing. I will check with Bella, and make sure she's happy to stay, but I really don't feel comfortable about Ellie, or Bella, for that matter, shooting off to an unknown destination in a dangerous flying cardboard box. It's a hare-brained idea and I just don't like it very much. I'm not sure I even want Harry involved!'

"Let's play dogs" (by Bella)

    'But we'll be back before you know we've gone!' said Harry. 'Please Mummy I MUST go and help the other cousins, I really must. I'm three weeks older than Bea, and if she gets to go, why can't I?'

Clare quite agreed that Harry was right. She realised she would be more than unpopular with him for a very, very long time if she didn't let him go, and besides she did want them all to find Ogo Pogo together. 'OK Harry, you can go' but I shall keep Bella and Ellie with me. They can play in the garden and I shall expect to see you back here... er... roughly at the time when you left – though how that works, beats me!' she laughed.

'Ooh là là!' quipped Harry (his current favourite expression) and he began to feel really excited!

'Right,' said Joe, 'Now you four come with me and we'll go and do some 'ESP' in my music room, and we'd better get on with it quickly.'

So the four of them ran to Joe's room and sat down. Joe told them to sit in a circle and hold hands and close their eyes. This way he linked everyone up together. He said this would add strength to the process. He asked them to breathe slowly and relax all their muscles. He asked them to slow down and concentrate their minds. Bea began to get the giggles when she heard Alex give a little burp, and Sophia was having trouble not laughing too. But Harry was straight into it right away. 'Come on, guys... concentrate!' he whispered as he remembered how his favourite football players always did stuff like this before a match in order to focus.

'Now, all of you, I want you think about Ogo Pogo,' said Joe quietly. 'Focus your minds on that little chap and think about how you think he looks, how he sounds and try and get a real physical picture of him in your mind. Imagine him sitting in the cockpit of that Lego aeroplane flying through Alex's window. Imagine him smiling and happy.' There was a quite a long pause before Joe added 'Now then, ask Ogo, in your mind, where he is. Say to him, in your minds... *Where are you Ogo, give us a clue?*'

There was a good long hush as everyone asked Ogo, in their minds, where he was. Several long seconds passed.

Suddenly Harry gave a gasp of horror 'OH NO!' he exclaimed.

Chapter 8

Everyone immediately opened their eyes and looked at Harry. 'What is it?' they chorused.

'Wait a minute!' said Joe. Don't say anything just yet, Harry! Here are some papers and pens. I want each of you to draw or write down anything that came into your mind during that exercise, anything at all.'

They sat quietly for a few moments while they concentrated on their drawings.

'Right, what have we got?' asked Joe. Harry you'd better go first.'

'I'm sorry to say,' said Harry, 'that I saw some Lego, some red Lego. There were just a few pieces. They looked like the cockpit of an aeroplane. They were lying on the ground.'

'OK,' said Joe, 'hold onto that thought, but don't panic... It doesn't mean Ogo was in the aeroplane, or that he is in danger, or injured in any way.'

'Alex, what have you got?'

'Well, I don't know why really,' replied Alex, 'but I saw a lot of water. A river or the sea, or was it the river AND the sea? Anyway, it was rough with big waves and it was windy.'

'Bea, what about you?' asked Joe.

'Well, it's a bit unhelpful, Uncle Joe, but all I saw was a long length of stupid rope.'

'Not necessarily stupid,' said Joe. 'And Sophia what about you?'

'Well… Bit strange too, Uncle Joe, but all I could see were red and white stripes.'

'Hmm,' said Joe. That all makes a little sense I suppose.'

'Why! How can it!?' Sophia exclaimed.

'Right, well, let me explain. I want you to think of these as all your clues. They are like pieces of a jigsaw puzzle. You have got something to work with now, but there are some pieces missing. Part of the picture is there, but it doesn't make much sense – yet. But it might help you by telling you what I saw.

I actually saw Ogo Pogo perfectly OK, but calling to you from a great height, and he wants you to go and rescue him. He was shouting and waving, and the other clue was, that I clearly saw Aldeburgh Yacht Club. I think you must go straight there. I don't know what you might find, but it may be that Ogo's stuck up a mast, or in a boat with a striped sail, or on top of the Club House on the flag pole, with a red or white striped flag, or something. But that would definitely be my suggestion as a starting place. Do you agree?'

'Well, we've got to start somewhere!' said Alex wisely, 'and we've got absolutely no other clues.'

'But,' added Joe, 'I want you to take a length of rope with you. Bea saw that, and it may be needed, and I'm going to give you three more straws, one each, for your flying box. I've got a feeling that you'll all need all the help you can get. Now then, you go and get in the magic box

and get ready. I'll get the things you need, plus
some water to drink, some of those sandwiches,
apples, and nut bars to share for snacks.'

'Uncle Joe, I don't suppose you have a Swiss
army knife that we could borrow?' asked Alex. He
felt very empty-handed without any tools at all.
'Hmm. Let me have a look,' replied Joe, 'I must
have one somewhere!'

Without hesitating, the four children ran out
through the front door and wriggled into the box.
It almost felt like home to be there again. Harry
was amazed at the size of it inside. 'Why! It feels
quite spacious when you're inside doesn't it!'

'YES, Harry it's amazing!' they choroused, as
Joe returned with the things they needed. He
handed Alex his old Swiss army pen knife. 'Sorry
old chap, bit small and rusty but the best I've got
— not particularly good about tools, I'm afraid,
not like Uncle Tom!'

'I hope Bella will be alright on her own here
— I hope she won't mind not coming?' enquired
Bea.

'Don't worry about Bella, Bea. Clare said
Bella didn't want to come in the box. She said she
wants to stay and play with Ellie. And now she's so
busy playing, that when you get back, it will be as
if you hadn't gone! Off you go now! Don't forget
the magic words, tell the box where to go and
GOOD LUCK! Be brave! Be determined, take care
of each other, and be careful!'

'Bye, Uncle Joe, thank you, you ARE magic!'
shouted the children together.

Joe could hear the words being chanted by
the children:
'We play in the box,
'We play in the box,
'We play in the box,
All day!
Go to Aldeburgh Yacht Club!'
And suddenly the box had disappeared, and
Joe slowly made his way back up the path, lost in
childhood memories.

Wisps of cloud drifted past them and looked so nearby,
that the children felt they could have caught hold of them.

Chapter 9

Alex made three more little slits in the corners of the box with Uncle Joe's knife so that all four children could look down the straws. The box swerved off in a northerly direction, hugging the coast line to the east. They went past crying seagulls and calling birds. It was an amazing view seeing the town of Ipswich so far below, all the little houses and cars receding into the distance as the treetops and patchwork fields took precedence beneath them. The sea and river water gleamed and glinted in the sunlight on the lovely clear day. Wisps of clouds drifted past them and looked so nearby that the children felt they could have caught hold of them.

'Harry, what do you think all that ESP is about? I mean, what does having sixth sense mean?' asked Bea as she sat back in the box enjoying the ride.

'Well, let me see,' said Harry, who loved giving little talks on things. Settling into his subject he continued, 'You know that we have five senses: SIGHT, SMELL, TOUCH, SOUND and TASTE. And we use those senses every single day to get information to our brains.'

Harry continued 'but according to Daddy, there is one more sense that is a bit more difficult to describe. The sixth sense. It's the extra sense – just 'knowing' something without being told. Some people are more aware of their sixth sense because they are more 'tuned in' to their inside thoughts and feelings. They train themselves to listen inside. That's what all that yoga and meditation is for. Some people even learn to read each other's thoughts without speaking.'

'Ooh, that's called telepathy,' said Alex excitedly. 'I read about that in my Guinness Book of Records. It's like two people communicating with each other on their mobiles but without words and without handsets!'

'WOW!' said Bea. 'That's SO cool. That could be really awesome and useful. I wonder how we can make that work? It could come in handy couldn't it – today even? Suppose we get split up and want to send each other some tele – thingy. Could we do that?'

'Well,' said Harry. We would probably need to practice 'tuning in' to ourselves and to each other quite a bit!'

'Let's try it!' said Sophia excitedly. 'Let's all do that thing we did with Joe. We'll hold hands and go inside ourselves and listen to our sixth sense. Then Bea, you start thinking very VERY hard of something and we'll try and tune in to what that is. OK?'

So, the four of them sat hand in hand and closed their eyes and went very quiet.

But in only a little while, Bea gave a snort and started giggling. She couldn't control herself. She started giggling so much that she couldn't stop, and then she started laughing and laughing and it was so infectious, that soon they were all rolling about in the bottom of the box in uncontrollable peals of laughter, tears, gulps and hiccups.

'Oh, stop it Bea!' shouted Sophia, 'you're giving me a tummy ache!' as the tears of laughter rolled down her cheeks.

Gradually they calmed down again.

'Well, anyway, Bea, I knew exactly what you were thinking about,' said Alex. 'My sixth sense told me perfectly, so there!'

'Really?' said Bea 'what was it then, clever clogs?'

'You were thinking about those nut bars and how you wanted to eat one.'

Bea took in a sharp intake of breath. 'He's right!' she whispered. And everyone went very silent.

To Framlingham
Kettleburgh   Parham

Snape

Thorpeness

Little Japan

Aldeburgh

Blaxhall

Iken

Slaughden
Aldeburgh
Yacht Club

The Woods

Butley Mills

Martello
Tower

Butley

Orford

R. Alde

Orford
Lighthouse

Orford Ness

Orford Beach

To Nacton

R. Ore

N

Shingle Street

Chapter 10

The children changed the subject and looked down their straws.

'Oh, look!' they cried, 'we can see the sea AND the river!'

Sure enough, as they gazed downwards, they could see how they were heading north along the coastline, leaving the sea to the right as they went. The river wound along beside the sea. It glinted like a slithery snake in the sunshine and the sea looked grey and vast with white speckles and ripples on top of it. Down below the river looked SO close to the sea at times and when it got to Aldeburgh town with the clusters of houses and the church, the river looked like it almost joined the sea just before it turned sharply at an angle, widening like a fat balloon, westwards, inland.

'Gosh it's close to the sea, isn't it?' shouted Bea. 'Look, there's the Martello Tower!'

'And look, that's when the river goes inland to Iken!' said Alex. 'I know that because we go there sometimes in the speed boat, for picnics (if we don't go to Little Japan).'

'Oh yes! And we sometimes go on to Snape where the river comes to an end,' added Sophia.

'Well, it doesn't end there, it's actually a bit further on under the Snape Bridge where the river actually STARTS! True fact, Soph!'

But Sophia had lost interest in the details... and was looking carefully through her straw.

'Look, guys, we're nearly there! Where shall we land? We don't want anyone to see us and we don't want anyone to steal our flying box!'

'How about parking up near Gar Gar's little shell beach beyond the South Start — you know the place she takes us to look for shells and sea glass, and to give Bunty a swim,' Harry suggested. 'It's a good place — people don't go there much. There's that mountain of rubbish that the yacht club dump near there - old furniture, bits of wood etc., and our box wouldn't look out of place especially if we could tuck it out of sight.'

So that's what they did. They neatly landed their box by the little beach and wriggling out of it, dragged it up out of sight behind the rubbish heap.

'RIGHT! So, now what do we do? What's our plan?' asked Bea.

'Well,' said Alex, 'we've got SOME clues to go on, though they are a bit vague, wild and weird. Joe suggested Ogo Pogo might be stuck up a mast, or up a flag pole or something. He saw him as high up. We know we've got to look out for Sophia's clue — something red and white striped and, well, we are already actually by the sea and the river which was my clue, so that's a start. Harry, did you see anything else apart from some red Lego, I mean was it anywhere in particular?'

'Hmm,' replied Harry, 'thinking about it, it was lying on the ground, amongst a load of stones or shingle if I remember rightly. But that could be absolutely anywhere – so not much help I'm afraid.'

'I agree that's all a bit vague. But why don't we split up and search the area?' Sophia suggested. 'Bea and I could go and scout around the Club House while you boys check out round the Martello tower, the South Start shed and Dinghy Park. Look for anything red and white, at the top of masts or flag poles and keep our eyes peeled for that tiny little fellow!'

'OK, that's a plan!' said Harry. 'We'll start up at Martello and make our way to the Club House. Suggest we meet there in 15 minutes? OK?'
Sophia and Bea ran as fast as they could to the clubhouse. They galloped along at top speed. They skirted round the back of the Club House, checked in the lost property box on the way and then dashed up the metal fire escape steps at the side of the Club House to the bridge.

'Shhh, try not to clank as we go! We're not supposed to go up these steps, Soph!' panted Bea as they climbed up.

'No, I know,' whispered Sophia, 'but look — no one's about really, everyone's downstairs inside the clubhouse having lunch – and we simply MUST have a look around especially at the top of the flag poles. We'll be as quick as poss. Bea can you keep an eye out through the window for people coming up the inside stairs, while I look around the bridge itself?'

They nipped around the corner at the top of the fire escape onto the bridge. Bea kept half an eye on the entrance through the sliding door and Sophia scrutinised all the flags and the flag poles. 'Oh, bother!' muttered Sophia 'All the flags have been lowered down and put away and there's no sign of anything at all.'

'Where are the flags kept?' whispered Bea.

'They're just in there,' said Sophia, 'Look, they're all rolled up and put away in that wooden cubby hole thing.' And very daringly, she quietly slid open the sliding door and crept into the Bridge room. The flags all looked neat and tidy; she examined them all carefully but there was not much to see apart from the red and white of some of the class flags. 'This is not really what I saw,' said Sophia. 'When I saw my clue, the red and white stripes were sort of spread out and nothing was shaped like a flag.'

They took in the long narrow room full of light and an enormous vista. There were four high stools in a row tucked under the long desk in front of the window, with excellent views of the river all around. There were pads of paper, pens and racing rules neatly stacked along the desk.

'Gosh, it's brilliant in here — see all those pairs of binoculars! Look!' And taking up a pair, Sophia peered through them, surveying the river, left and right. 'I can see for miles!' She scanned all the tops of the masts in the dinghy park, and the flag poles in front of her.

Bea picked up a pair too, and adjusting them, squinted at the surrounding area. 'Oh, look! There are Alex and Harry! They're coming this way, looking under and around everything. I suppose that means they haven't found Ogo yet.' she whispered.

'Oh heck, what ARE we going to do next?' asked Sophia.

'Well, Sophia, I have got an idea that might help,' said Bea seriously, adding, 'I am just wondering if it would be actually 'stealing' if we just borrowed a pair of these binoculars. We would definitely put them back. If Ogo Pogo is somewhere high up, it might be a lot easier to see him if we could use the binoculars to look for him.'

Sophia thought for a minute. 'Hmmm. I think we could write a note to the Officer of the day, stating that we have borrowed a pair of binoculars, that we will bring them back and sign it. That might not be so bad. There's a smaller pair up there on the shelf. Perhaps we could borrow those ones — they might not need them. I'll write a note and sign it Rose P., then they will think it was Mummy. I'm sure that would be OK — after all, she IS on the sailing committee.' Sophia spoke in low tones. 'I expect she would be a bit cross if she knew, though, but hopefully she will never know'. She wrote in her best handwriting on the pad.

Dear Offisir ov the day. I have burrowed some bnoklars and will bring them back later. Signed Rose P.

'Right, come on Bea, let's scarper out of here and go and find the boys.' And with that they quietly went back out onto the bridge, slid the door shut and nimbly scooted down the fire escape with the pair of binoculars hidden under Sophia's jacket.

They collected four cups of cold water from the water fountain and made their way into the Club House which was full of noisy grownups with loud shouty voices all talking at once. There was the clattering of plates, knives and forks and general hubbub.

Alex and Harry were sitting on one of the benches by the glass doors. They looked pretty fed up. Sophia and Bea handed them the water, which they drank thirstily, and explained that they too had not found anything at all. Sophia kept the binoculars hidden in her jacket – she didn't want to show them to Alex or Harry in the Club House. They sat there swinging their legs, looking absently around them. No one took any notice of the four children, they were well known. Everyone would assume that their parents were in the lunch queue.

Sophia got off the bench and wandered over to the wall opposite with all the sailing photos on it. Something had grabbed her attention. It was strange – as if she had seen something that she needed to examine closer.

Suddenly she rushed back to the others and exclaimed. 'Oh my God! There's something I simply HAVE to show you! But shhh — don't make a fuss!' And she put her finger to her lips.

Orfordness Lighthouse 1975

Chapter 11

The four of them sauntered nonchalantly over to the wall on the other side of the room and Sophia pointed to one of the old framed photos. All over the wall there was a gallery of many old photos of yachts, people, and sailing events, in ancient sepia, monotone and also coloured. But Sophia was pointing to a particular photo. It was of a lighthouse. It was in faded colour — red and white striped, tall, imposing and set on a surrounding beach in a white clouded blue sky, against a grey river. Underneath the photo an inscription read ORFORDNESS LIGHTHOUSE 1975.

'That's it! That's what I saw!' whispered Sophia in awe. 'Those were what the stripes looked like in my clue! I'm absolutely sure of it!'

Alex nudged the others and indicated that they should go outside.

They jumped down the back stairs and assembled by the lost property box.

'Right, Sophia! Are you 100% convinced?' asked Alex sternly. 'We need to know for sure.'

Sophia studied the ground, shuffling the gravel with the toe of her trainer for a minute, thinking hard. 'Now look here, Alex, you've got to believe me, all I know is that that picture on the wall grabbed my attention immediately. It seems absolutely right. It is exactly the sort of stripes I saw, the right colours and everything. Maybe my sixth sense has kicked in, maybe it's ESP, but I've got an absolutely weird feeling that that lighthouse is the last missing clue.'

'Well, apart from the bit of Lego we still haven't found,' murmured Harry, looking disgruntled.

'Well,' said Bea, 'I believe in Sophia. She has been absolutely right with everything she's said up to now. Since we haven't got any better ideas, and no other clues, why don't we just get on with it, and get to the Orfordness Lighthouse — wherever that is — as soon as we can. It's not a problem, we've got the flying box and we've got some rope, Alex's pen knife and... Oh! And by the way, I'm STARVING, can we eat those nut bars now?'

The three others giggled at this. 'Good idea Bea!' they chorused.

'Wait a minute!' said Harry. 'I wonder if Orford lighthouse is on rocks on the opposite side of the river from Orford quay. When the tide's high it's pretty difficult to get close to it. I think you have to go by boat. You know Orford, it's where we go for lunch sometimes at that pub. You know, we often go crabbing over the quayside. But how the heck are we going to get the box onto a lighthouse?' Harry paused for more thought, then continued, 'We can't exactly land it on the top, and it doesn't have sticky feet to stick to the sides! I reckon the rocks directly at the bottom of the lighthouse are only accessible by boat by sea, and we don't have a boat. Do we?' Harry added.

'RIGHT!' declared Alex. 'I've absolutely had

enough of all this faffing about and all this talking. It's time we actually achieved something. There's just too much talk and not enough action! COME ON! Follow me!'

And lifting the lid of the lost property trunk, he dived headfirst into it, poked about and came out with four old jackets which he handed the girls and Harry, three battered old sailing caps and four rather old smelly lifejackets. 'Put them on... Good! Right! Let's go!'

Alex dashed back up the dinghy park past the South Start and back to their magic flying box.

'Get in everyone!' he shouted, and nobody disobeyed him, though they hadn't got a clue what he was doing.

Sophia showed Harry and Alex the binoculars. 'Great!' said Harry, 'those could come in really useful!'

Alex continued, 'Grab the rope Bea and coil it round your shoulder so that it's secure. I've got Joe's Swiss army knife. Right everyone... Magic words, please!'

'We play in the box,
We play in the box,
We play in the box,
All day!' they chanted.

'Take us to the rib!' shouted Alex.

The rib was Jon, Tom and Joe's rubber dinghy with an outboard engine. It was on a mooring just beyond the Elbow Buoy on the wall side of the river.

At Alex's instruction, the box instantly took off and flew away along the river. It landed neatly in the back of the rubber rib just behind the driver's seat. Everyone scrambled out with difficulty.

'Ooh gosh, that was tricky with so little space to move!' said Harry. 'What's the plan Alex?'

'We are jolly well going to go to Orford in the rib, and I'm driving it!'

Everyone gave a gasp.

Now, Alex was actually pretty proficient at driving the rib and the children knew that. There was only one small problem, which is that they ABSOLUTELY, definitely wouldn't be allowed EVER to have gone alone without an adult driver. But Alex reckoned 'needs must' and didn't bother to worry about the consequences — for the moment. *I'll worry about all that later*, he thought to himself.

'Now sit up tall, everyone! Put your caps and jackets on and look like grown-ups. We'll go slowly down the far side of the river until we get past the Club House. Hopefully everyone is still downstairs having their noisy lunch. Soph, keep an eye out to the bridge with your binoculars. Harry, can you get up front and untie the painter to the buoy–that's that rope tied to it- good, now throw it into the bow of the rib. Now let's go! Harry, can you sit at the front and keep an eye out. Bea and Soph, you're best sitting in the stern there. Maybe try to keep the box dry if you can – look, here's an old towel to throw over it!'

And with that Alex reached into the locker under the driver's seat and got the key. He attached the 'kill chord' to his wrist and turned the ignition. The rib propeller turned over just once, and the engine started. Vrrooom! They motored quietly and steadily up the far bank of the river. Alex was careful not to go too close to the mud on the bank as Jon had taught him. He sat up tall in the driver's seat; with the buoyancy aid and jacket he looked quite bulky. He had put on Jon's spare sunglasses and the cap. It was a good disguise and no one shouted at them from the Club House veranda.

At the South Start, Alex steered the boat into the middle of the river knowing that it would be quicker to motor there, as the tide was going out, and would take them along. All the children were quiet. They knew Alex had to concentrate but they did have faith in his driving as he'd done it so often.

Suddenly they heard a shout from the bank in front of the Martello tower. Someone was waving madly at them and calling.

'Oh no!' they groaned, 'We've been found out.'

'Who is it, Sophia — can you see with those binoculars?' shouted Harry.

'Oh crikey!' exclaimed Sophia and Bea together. 'It's Gar Gar and Bunty!'

Gar Gar had been walking Bunty along the bank of the river, just as she often did at lunchtimes. Bunty had spotted the rib, seen the children and jumped headlong into the river.

Gar Gar was shouting and waving furiously and they just made out her words as they drifted across the river…

'Jon! Please take Bunty with you!' And sure enough, looking closely, they could see Bunty swimming towards the rib for all she was worth. Her black ears were flapping on the top of the waves. Bunty adored going with the grandchildren anywhere and often jumped into the river to follow the boat. She hated being left behind.

'Gargs thinks you're Jon, Alex! And you know her eyesight is SO appallingly dreadful… we might get away with it. Give her the thumbs up,' instructed Sophia.

Without hesitating and at the top of her loudest voice Sophia yelled, 'OK GARGS, WE'LL TAKE HER, AND BRING HER BACK TO YOUR HOUSE LATER! DON'T WORRY!'

'OK thanks!' shouted Gar Gar, and she waved them on.

'PHEW!' they chorused.

And with that, Harry, Sophia and Bea hauled a very bedraggled Bunty into the front of the rib, threw the towel over her, and tried to dry her while Bunty went wild with enthusiasm, wagging her wet tail, wriggling and jumping all over the place, getting everyone very wet.

Bunty wriggled and jumped all over the place (by Ellie)

'EUGH! BUNTY! STOP IT!' they squealed. 'SIT DOWN, we're all getting soaked!' It was a right old muddle... But Sophia and Harry took control. 'BUNTY, SIT!' said Sophia assertively. With that Bunty plopped down on her bottom, panting, hung her tongue out of her mouth, smiled and looked extremely pleased with herself.

'Oh, for goodness' sake... I have no idea what on earth we're going to do with Bunty,' remarked Bea. 'She's not going to be much help at all – she can be such a menace!' And she folded her arms nervously. Secretly she was a bit worried and a tiny bit cross. 'How on earth is Bunty going to fit in the magic box?' she continued. They all shrugged; there was absolutely no solution to that question.

Alex opened up the throttle and pushed forward the control until the dial reached 30 mph. The water spray was white and frothy as they zoomed southwards in the direction of Orford and Shingle Street. The water was cold — it was only

early summer and had not warmed up properly.
The children were grateful for the extra jackets,
even though they did smell old and salty. It was
always a challenge going in the rib; they nearly
always got wet, and it was particularly chilly in
the front. Harry was very uncomplaining as he
cuddled closer to a very damp Bunty. In the end
he even stuck his head under the wet towel.

The good thing is that they were all used to
it. They had all done this trip numerous times and
knew it took only seven minutes or so to get
there, at top speed.

"Please take Bunty!"
shouted Gar Gar

Chapter 12

They sped along to Orford. As they went through the moorings, Alex slowed down and chugged along sedately between the boats.

'Look! There's the lighthouse... but it's way over there on the other side of the spit by the sea. See?! It's right on that bank of shingle. We can't get to it from here, not by boat, anyway. We have to go out of the mouth of the river and then double back along the shore near to the beach to get close to it.'

'Oh NO Alex, that's miles along — it will take us ages,' said Sophia anxiously. 'Can't we land here and walk across — or fly across in the magic box?'

'No Soph, I'm afraid I don't think we can do that,' explained Alex. 'We can't leave Bunty in the rib by herself and I really don't think we'll get her in the box very easily. We're too visible from Orford quay anyway. There's nowhere to tie up the rib. Also, it must be a good forty-minute walk to the lighthouse from here.'

'Look there's a notice — dogs aren't allowed on National Trust land either. It's all very difficult,' added Harry.

'Oh dear!' cried Bea, 'I knew Bunty would be a nuisance.'

'Don't worry Bea, it'll be OK, just hang on!'

And with that Alex motored along through the moorings on the other side of Orford, opened up the throttle again and sped along heading for the mouth of the river at Shingle Street. They passed Havergate Island and carried on down the river with the shingle bank on the port side of the rib.

It wasn't long before it began to get rougher as they approached the sea. The convergence of the river and the sea created swirls and currents, eddies and waves. The breeze was against them but the river was taking them out to sea at great speed. Alex, anticipating ahead, did not like the look of the greying sky and squalling winds that were approaching. He glanced at his wristwatch. It was coming up to 2.30pm. He remembered that this was often a time when the wind strengthened for no accountable reason that he knew of. Although the tide was under them, the opposing gale was now creating sizeable waves against the current. A well-known thing; wind against tide. Not easy to navigate. The wind began to howl as the rib bounced up and down on the ever-increasing crashing waves. Awash with water, the rib rode high on the peaks and then lurched down again into a valley of surging cold water. Harry and Bunty were getting really drenched in the front.

Harry was brave and gritted his teeth against the almighty splashing and dousing that were coming his way. He held on tightly to Bunty.

'BEA!' he yelled in-between gusts, 'throw me that rope of yours!' Bea threw the coil and Harry caught it. He lassoed Bunty round her middle with the rope and then tied the other end to his wrist.

He reckoned she'd be safer if she was tied to him. He was really cold now and it took all his courage not to shout at Alex to STOP!

The girls were shivering inside their jackets; they clung onto each other and the magic box through the spray and wind but no one dared say anything. They were biting their lips.

Only Alex ignored all the weather. His mouth was set in a straight line as he clenched his lips to stop his teeth chattering in the freezing wind. He was determined to keep going through all this rough tidal weather until they had made it out into the sea where he hoped it would be calmer. He knew that there were spits and islands of shingle to navigate, but as the tide was still pretty high, he reckoned the rib should be OK. Through the wind and spray he could just about make out the mounds of shingle ahead. Small islands of pebbles raised up out of the water. Veering to the left he headed to what he thought was a clear deep channel of water between them. 'HANG ON, EVERYONE!' he yelled as he swung the steering wheel to the left. The boat lunged forwards, and seemed to be shifting through the turgid water when it slowed down for a moment. There was a terrible CRUNNNNCH and grinding as the propeller hit shingle and the rib came to a sudden halt. The engine stalled.

'ALEX! LOOK OUT!' shouted Sophia.

And then all the children screamed as the rib tipped on its side. The propeller had got stuck in some shingle on the edge of a small mound of pebbles sticking out of the sea. Alex had missed the deepest part of the channel by about 30 centimetres. Everyone was screaming and shouting. Sophia and Bea at the stern were hanging onto the magic box which was sliding sideways down towards the water. Alex yelled: 'DON'T PANIC! QUICK EVERYONE, SCRAMBLE UP TO THIS SIDE OF THE RIB!' and the children crawled and moved their weight to the other side of the rib to try and right it.

There was a moment of silence as the rib righted itself a little, and then suddenly there was another scream from Bea: 'HARRY! BUNTY! THEY'VE DISAPPEARED! WHERE ARE THEY!?'

'OH MY GOD! LOOK!' shouted Sophia as she pointed across the water.

There, floundering in the waves with his arms thrashing, the lifejacket turning him this way and that, was Harry. He was bobbing up and down, being dashed by the waves and currents, but he could not begin to swim in any direction. There next to him tied to his wrist was Bunty whose legs were working very hard to stay afloat. She was coughing and spitting as she valiantly tried to keep herself from drowning. They had both been catapulted out of the bow of the rib in the sudden crash onto the shingle.

'HELP!' They could hear Harry shouting! 'HELP! SAVE ME!' and his voice grew fainter and fainter as he was carried further and further away from them.

He was being swept along by the tide, which was fast and furious. He was a good swimmer, but nothing would prepare a 7½year-old for the undertow of currents that he was enduring now. His head kept bobbing under the water. He was choking and spluttering as he was carried, along with Bunty, ever further and further away towards the open sea. And the tide was rushing out now and there was no catching him.

The wind began to howl (by Bea)

Chapter 13

'QUICK! Bea, sit here and hold onto the steering wheel. Soph, jump out with me onto the shingle! We've got to push this boat off!'
So, Alex and Sophia slithered down the side of the rubber rib and jumped onto the mound of stones. It was only a small area of shingle but the propeller was caught in it. Alex tried to clear a small trench round it with his foot, but it was not easy in 20 centimetres of water. 'OK, Sophia,' shouted ALEX. 'Come to the front up here. We need to push her off backwards. When I say GO, we PUSH like MAD and Bea, be ready to turn on the engine. Ready? PUSH!'

Sophia and Alex pushed for all they were worth. The rib moved a little but not enough to get it off the stones. 'IT'S NO GOOD, ALEX,' yelled Sophia into the wind, exasperated. 'IT'S TOO HEAVY – we're not strong enough! Oh HELP! We MUST HURRY TO SAVE HARRY AND BUNTY!'

'BEA, jump down and help!' shouted Alex. So, Bea slid down and stood at the front, all of them together. Alex got hold of the rib's painter and then counted... '1, 2, 3, PUSH!' The three of them pushed with all their strength and the rib slowly slid off the stones and shifted into the channel with Alex hanging onto it with the rope.

'RIGHT, QUICK! UP you get!' And exerting himself, he heaved and shoved Bea and Sophia back into the rib and climbed up himself. By now the rib was drifting into the main stream of the channel towards the sea. They could just about make out Harry and Bunty bobbing about on the waves ahead of them. They looked very small. Alex turned the key and mercifully the engine started. He pushed the lever forwards and gingerly he manoeuvred the rib into the water along the channel between the shingle mounds. Increasing the throttle gradually, he was soon making good progress at a moderate speed. Harry and Bunty were ahead of them almost out of the channel nearly in the sea waters. They could see Harry was still kicking about and waving his arm, but they weren't sure about Bunty.

'Thank goodness he's wearing a lifejacket!' said Bea through clenched teeth as she was showered with cold spray.

They gained on Harry and were soon able to make out what was happening. It seemed that Bunty was swimming strongly at an angle against the tide, valiantly trying to make for one of the little islands of shingle. She was literally pulling Harry along who was trying to help by kicking his legs. But the lifejacket, though keeping him afloat, was also hindering his progress with its bulk. Bunty was working hard to pull him to safety.

'BUNTY'S SAVING HARRY!' yelled Sophia.

The rib caught up with Harry and Bunty. Harry was spluttering and choking. Bunty was flagging, looking very tired indeed.

'ALRIGHT, HARRY?' shouted Alex. 'Let's get you out of here! Grab this!'   And coiling the rope he swung it into the water and Harry grabbed it with his other hand. Hand over hand, Alex pulled Harry who in turn was pulling Bunty towards the rib. As Harry got alongside, the two girls heaved him aboard and then they grasped Bunty by her shoulders and pulled her slithering and whimpering into the boat, looking like a shiny wet seal.

Alex said nothing but taking the wheel again, concentrated on swinging the boat round 180 degrees. He turned northwards again but this time along the shore line of the sea side of Shingle Street. He was heading for the light house.

"Alright Harry?" shouted Alex. "Let's get you out of here!"
(by Alex)

After the storm was over...

Chapter 14

Harry lay curled up in the bottom of the bow of the rib. He was absolutely exhausted. Sophia and Bea had covered him with their jackets and Bunty was curled up next to him. They had given him some water and a sandwich to eat. The shock was slowly subsiding. He bravely said he was 'fine'. He began to feel warm and cosy inside and he started to doze. He had explained that Bunty had literally saved his life as she had pulled him towards safety and kept him going. 'She was a hero!' they all exclaimed.

Bunty was given extra pats and hugs and bits of nut bar which she gobbled up gleefully. She had a huge smile on her face and was so very proud of herself. Bea was extra-loving towards Bunty. Bea felt bad at having been so dismissive of her earlier. It seemed miraculous that neither Harry nor Bunty were much the worse for their ordeal.

As Alex motored northwards hugging the shore line, the wind seemed to have abated. They were no longer driving into it, so it was behind them, pushing them along, and the waves were smaller. The sun had come out again and they began to feel warm. Everyone felt better and happier. They could see the lighthouse some distance ahead of them up the beach on the port side of the rib. Everywhere was deserted. Being there was like being on the edge of the world.

'Let's ALL have something to eat,' said Sophia 'I'm famished!' And she grabbed the sandwiches, and passed one each round to Alex, and Bea along with the water bottle.

As they motored smoothly northwards along Orford beach, hugging the shore, they sat in silence munching their sandwiches, lost in their own thoughts. They could each imagine the horror that would have transpired if they had not managed to save Harry, or Bunty for that matter. They each knew that they had all been in real danger and that if anyone ever knew about it, they would be in serious trouble.

Alex was fully aware of the risk he had taken trying to get out of the mouth of the river when the tide was taking them that way. He shivered inside at the thought of what might have happened. He had heard stories before of sailors getting swept out to sea at Shingle Street. He was just SO grateful that they were all safe, that no one had been really hurt, injured or worse. And he was worried about getting them all back home in one piece too. He eyed up the approaching lighthouse with suspicion. How were they ever to find Ogo Pogo there? That's supposing Sophia was right in saying that the two red stripes she had seen were the ones on the lighthouse at all.

Alex felt weary and the weight of the responsibility of the whole adventure sat heavily in him. For the first time, he began to wish his Mummy and Daddy were there. Alex knew they would solve this problem much quicker and he knew his father would never have got them into such danger. He was disappointed in himself and did not feel confident about the outcome of their mission.

Sophia, for her part, was quietly thinking about what she could do now to help Alex. She could see how tired he was and was racking her brains as to what else she could do to make things easier. But bother! Nothing came. She felt drowsy, and her eye lids kept drooping as Bea snuggled up to her.

As Alex approached Orford Lighthouse he slowed down. There it was. Remote, isolated, 30 metres tall with two red stripes circling its circumference. Imposing. Deserted and desolate. Less than 10 metres away from the edge of the sea. Undermined by coastal erosion. No longer in use. Doomed to extinction within the next year or two. Two white painted huts next to it, a bench, and a little whitewashed rectangular porch doorway to get into the tower. Shingle and bleached shells, with washed up pieces of flotsam and jetsam scattered around it.

He pulled up alongside the lighthouse and indicated to Sophia to come to the bow of the boat. Manoeuvring alongside the shingle, he cut the engine.

Sophia jumped down with the painter onto the beach and dragged the boat into the shore. There was little in the way of waves now and everything suddenly felt deliciously quiet and still. Silence. Bea and Alex slithered out down the side of the rubber leaving Harry and Bunty fast asleep in the front of the rib, recovering. Alex, Sophia and Bea pulled on the painter, unwound the anchor and wedged it into the shingle so that the rib was secure. Discarding their lifejackets and outer jackets, the three of them collapsed onto the warm pebbles.

It was simply beautiful; peaceful and relaxing with the sound of gentle lapping on the beach, the calling of a few lone seagulls winging away in the blue sky. A wave of exhaustion overcame the three of them and they lay back on the heated stones and instantaneously fell into a deep sleep.

They dreamed of exotic birds and flying dogs, leaping dolphins and monstrous waves, blue clouds, rainbow coloured skies and of little pixie-like creatures with arms, legs and tiny emerald green eyes.

Chapter 15

'Woof! Woof! WOOF! WOOF!' The sound of barking woke Sophia from her deep sleep with a jolt.

It was Bunty. She had jumped out of the rib and had run up near to the lighthouse, barking at it furiously, her tail wagging.

'Shhh! Bunty! STOP IT!' called Sophia as she jumped up and ran over towards the base of the lighthouse where Bunty was sitting.

'What is it, girl? Whatever is the matter?' Sophia, shading her eyes, peered upwards to where Bunty was looking, but she couldn't see what the dog was fussing about. Squinting upwards all she could see was the tall cylindrical lighthouse towering above her with its two red stripes. 'Now look here, Bunty, shhh be quiet, or you'll wake the others up!' she said assertively.

Bea stirred. Rubbing her eyes, she saw Sophia trying to squint upwards to the lighthouse. Bea ran back to the rib. Leaning in and grabbing the binoculars from the back seat, she then sprinted over to Sophia. 'What's going on Sophia?'

'I'm not sure Bea, Bunty is barking at something but I have no idea what.'

'Shall we wake up the others, Soph? Or just have a scout around here and let them sleep on?'

'Yes, let's just leave them for a bit longer and see what we can find round here. Keep a look out for Ogo - don't forget he's very small, and we don't want to tread on him!'

The two girls circled round the base of the light house. Bea peered through the binoculars looking up and down through them. They scanned the lighthouse base and kept looking upwards as they went. Sophia kept hoping she might find the Ogo Pogo or at least some clue to where he might be. The lighthouse looked so tall to the small girls, appearing to stretch miles upwards. Bunty was accompanying them sniffing around with great enthusiasm, tail wagging.

'She seems to be looking for something too!' exclaimed Bea. 'Remember, Joe said that he saw Ogo Pogo as 'high up' didn't he, Soph? I wonder if somehow or other we have to get up there and see if Ogo's at the top, or IN the top of the lighthouse.'

'Hmm, golly that's a thought,' replied Sophia. 'I wonder if it's possible to get inside and go up the stairs. I've seen pictures of lighthouses and I know they have winding stairs to the top so that the lighthouse keepers can go up there and attend to the light. Shall we try the door?'

Sophia and Bea walked round to the rectangular porch with the door to the lighthouse. Bunty was sitting, wagging her tail, watching them with interest. It was a strong wooden door with a key hole. Sophia pulled at the handle to see if the door would open. 'Bother, it's locked!' she said.

They scouted around the door. They looked everywhere around for a hook or a sill or a ledge where the key could be hidden.

'Where's your key hidden at your house, Bea?' asked Sophia.

'Well, we have a key safe thingy,' replied Bea. 'What about you, Soph?'

'It's on a ledge in the shed, but I can't see any ledges round here. Let's think, Bea. People put keys under flower pots by their front doors, don't they? But there aren't any pots here.'

'Yes, or under big stones?' suggested Bea. 'Hang on a minute Sophia, there's quite a few big rocks and stones by the little hut over there, shall we look round there? Come on Bunty! Come and look with us. Seek, Bunty, seek!'

Bunty started sniffing around. Her tail was wagging backwards and forwards as she rooted around amongst the rocks and stones.

Alex and Harry sauntered over with their hands in their pockets, yawning.

'Hi Soph, hi Bea, what's going on?' said Harry sleepily.

'Well, we want to get to the top of the lighthouse and were trying to find a key to get in so that we could look upstairs for Ogo,' answered Sophia.

'I suspect whoever owns it has their key with them at home,' suggested Harry.

'Well, we can still look!' replied Sophia, slightly exasperated.

So, the four of them and Bunty paced around the outbuildings, around the lighthouse looking under rocks and stones really carefully, upturning anything that looked like it could hide a key.

86

Suddenly Bunty gave a bark and went running over to Harry with something in her mouth, wagging her tail furiously. It was something red and plastic.

'Harry! What's she got? Has she found a key?' the others called out curiously.

'She's found the Lego!! She's really found it!!' shouted Harry with huge excitement. 'Oh BUNTY, GOOD GIRL! Clever girl! Now, DROP!' he said with assertion. And for once in her life, Bunty sat down and neatly deposited the Lego at Harry's feet on the ground.

'WOW! That's SO cool Harry! It's the last piece of the puzzle!' said Bea.

Sophia, shading her eyes, peered upwards
to where Bunty was looking.

Chapter 16

Harry was beaming from ear to ear while he patted and cuddled Bunty praising her and calling her a clever girl. He had secretly been disappointed that they hadn't found his clue before. It had felt like the missing part of the 'jigsaw' that his Daddy had talked about. It was a really happy moment for him.

They sat on the bench leaning against the whitewashed shed, and studied the piece. It had clearly come from the cockpit of Alex's Lego plane. 'I know that bit,' said Alex.

'But one thing's for sure,' he added with relief, 'we definitely are on the right track now, and in the right place! But it has been very hard so far, hasn't it?'

'I nearly drowned! And Bunty too!' exclaimed Harry, 'I've never been so scared in my life. It was dangerous. But at the same time, it has been really exciting and everyone's done their best, just like in a real team — and you've been very brave, Alex!'

'But not as much as you, Harry, and it was my fault you and Bunty nearly got lost at sea,' replied Alex, adding, 'I'm so sorry — I had no idea it would be so dangerous to go to the mouth of the river.'

'Look,' said Harry, 'You did your absolute best, Alex — you weren't to know there was a storm brewing, and at least we are all here now safely. We've got a mission to complete and we must be determined to do it, and need to concentrate on that.'

Harry was secretly thinking about how football team managers talk to their teams to make them play better. He looked at them all and added, 'I don't think we should ever tell anyone what happened to me and Bunty. Especially NEVER tell any of the grownups about it. If they knew the dangers we've been through, they'll make it more difficult for us to do things we want to do on our own in the future.'

'I agree,' nodded Bea. 'Let's keep that a secret shall we, just amongst ourselves? Do you agree everyone?'

'AGREED!' They all nodded and put one flat palm on top of each other's hand as a sign of a promise.

'So now what?' asked Harry, 'we need to get into the light house somehow or other and there doesn't seem to be a key to the padlock.'

Alex suddenly remembered something, and putting his hand in his pocket came out with Uncle Joe's rusty old Swiss army knife. He opened it up and examined all the various parts. He was rather impressed with the range he could see. He gave a low whistle. 'Wow! Not bad at all — good old Uncle Joe! I don't think he realized how cool this is!' Splaying them out, he could see a large blade, small blade, a nail file/nail cleaner, little pair of scissors, a metal file, metal saw, tiny screw driver, can opener, magnifying glass, and stainless-steel pin.

'Yep, now let me see…' And approaching the door, Alex inserted the stainless-steel pin into its key hole. He wriggled and twisted it several times this way and that, until suddenly, miraculously, there was a click as the lock sprang open. He turned the handle and the door began to open.

Bunty sat by the door, sweeping the ground with her wagging tail, looking on with interest, her ears cocked.

The door creaked and groaned on its rusty hinges as if it was irritated at being opened. The children peered inside. It was a little gloomy and dark. There was a smell of oil and damp, cold and salt. There were cobwebs around the doorway.

Straight ahead of them was a large downstairs room with two concrete spiralling staircases, one on either side of it. The stairs had dark green metal railings. A large dark green metal pole reached up right through the middle of the tower. Harry thought it looked a bit like a fireman's pole. As their eyes adjusted to the gloom, the children could see that the walls were whitewashed but with mustard coloured paint from waist height downwards. The stairs converged on the first landing and after that there was just one set going up and around the interior walls of the building. There were a few narrow windows on the way up and a larger window on each of the two landings. It was all so intriguing, the shape, the structure, the shell-like spiral. It was rather beautiful inside. A soft glow emanated from the top of the tower as the light spread downwards.

'Wow, it's cool!' exclaimed Bea. 'Come on, let's go up!'

So, the children began their ascent up the spiralling staircase. It seemed a long way. 30 metres is quite a climb, and the steps were steep. The higher they climbed, the steeper and narrower they became. There was a certain amount of huffing and puffing as up they went! The sunlight, where it shone through the windows, cast bright rectangles on the otherwise shady walls. As they went up and glanced through the windows, they were struck by the incredible views and vistas. SO much sea, land and space. It was awesome.

At last they reached the final narrow steps to the top room with its lead paned windows. Light poured into the spacious circular room through the criss-crossing glass all around. Outside was a small balcony like a girdle for the tower. It had railings with beautiful scallop-like nobs on top of each post. It was so incredible. All the children gave a gasp. The room was a brilliant white, full of sunshine and blue light all around them. Looking out of the windows they could see the arc of the coast line for miles, both north and south. There was a view for miles across the sea to the east; to the west they could see Orford castle, and the town of Aldeburgh with its church on the hill, in the distance. Bea looked through the binoculars around her neck. She was mesmerized — it was so fantastic. They could hear the peaceful sound of the waves down below and looking out to sea felt the immensity of it, its power and its inevitable domination of the coastline.

'Gosh I feel very small' exclaimed Harry. 'Imagine being up here on a rough night with the sea pounding and the wind blowing. I expect the lighthouse absolutely rocked about in a storm. It must have been quite scary! It's very sad it's not used nowadays isn't it?'

Come on now, everyone! said Sophia. 'We MUST find Ogo Pogo. Now watch where you tread, he's only little!' she added.

Everyone looked carefully all over the floor of the room and all along the joints with the walls. But they could see nothing. They were beginning to get desperate.

'Oh! I'm getting so frustrated!' remarked Sophia. 'I WISH we could find him.'

Suddenly Alex gave a yelp 'Look! Look! Out of the window! THERE HE IS! There's Ogo Pogo!'

And sure enough, there, outside, attached to piece of metal which protruded from the side of the tower, was a very small creature, with skinny arms and legs, a whirl of white hair and green eyes. Bea quickly examined the situation with the binoculars. Ogo was sitting astride the metal rods, holding on for dear life while waving feebly at them with his spare arm. He looked very tiny, very vulnerable and very, very tired.

'He's sitting on the lightning conductor!' exclaimed Alex. 'That's to divert the lightning from striking the lighthouse on a stormy night. Scary thought!'

'Oh my God!' Sophia cried. 'But how on earth are we going to get him? He's dangling outside, and we're inside, and I can't see how we're to get out there!'

Chapter 17

Harry looked thoughtful. 'I've got an idea!' he said. 'We could get in the magic box and fly up there, reach Ogo and scoop him up. Do you think the box could sort of 'hover' near or under something, Alex?'

'Well, I don't know,' Alex replied, 'but I guess we could try. Though the last thing we want to do, is make him fall to the ground from that lightning conductor.'

'Well, we haven't got any other options,' said Sophia. 'He could fall anyway any minute, he looks so exhausted.'

'You're right,' said Bea. Through the binoculars she could clearly see Ogo's little eyes drooping and he kept wobbling and wavering as if he couldn't hold himself up much longer. 'COME ON! HURRY!' shouted Bea.

The four of them clattered down the coiling stairway and out into the bright sunshine. They scarpered across the shingle back to the boat.

'Quick! Help me get the box out, Soph,' said Alex. He and Sophia scrambled up and into the stern of the rib and, grasping the box, hauled it back over the bow onto the sea shore. They all wriggled into it.

'Wait a minute!' yelled Bea and she scrambled out and made a dash back to the rib. She came back coiling the damp rope and handed it to Alex.

'Good idea, Bea,' said Alex, 'right now! Are we ready?' And they all chanted:

'We play in the box,
We play in the box,
We play in the box,
All day!'

'Take us to the light house and hover near the lightning conductor,' added Alex.

The box swung up quickly, climbing higher and ever higher as it approached the lighthouse. It circled round the top of the lighthouse and came to a halt above the lightning conductor.

The children peered at little Ogo through their straws. They could see him clearly, but they were unable to reach him from inside the box. 'Oh bother, said Sophia, 'the box is upright and we can't get him — even if we went underneath him, we wouldn't be able to reach up far enough.'

There was a silence as they each racked their brains to think of a plan.

'I've got an idea!' shouted Sophia. 'You must help me climb out of the top of the box with the rope tied round my waist. You three hang onto the end of the rope (and don't let go!) and lower me down to the lightning conductor and I'll get Ogo.'

'WHAT?! Sophia – that's FAR too dangerous!' they all cried. 'Suppose you fall?'

'Well, I'm not going to fall if I'm tied on, and you keep hold of the end of the rope,' replied Sophia stubbornly. 'Look, I'm good at this sort of thing. I do it at gymnastics, and I'm not in the least bit scared.'

So that's what they did. High up in the air, hovering over a metal conductor, the three children tied the rope securely round Sophia's waist, and then hoisted her up to the top of the magic box. She swung one leg over the side and then the other. She grasped hold of the rope with both hands and instructed the others to slowly lower her down the side. She could hear grunts of exertion coming from inside the box as the three children held onto the rope for dear life.

After a little while, Sophia was swinging free from the box bottom. She didn't dare look downwards — as she swung 30 metres in the air like a trapeze artist. She shouted at them to lower her down a bit more and in a little while she was parallel to the lightning conductor. Reaching out with one arm, she pulled herself in towards it until she was close to Ogo Pogo.

'Hello little Ogo,' she said quietly. 'Don't you worry about a thing now. You're going to be just fine. I'm going to reach out and take you in my hand and put you in my pocket and zip you up safe. Is that OK?' Sophia was so soothing and calming – so excellent with little creatures.

Ogo Pogo gave a little squeak and nodded his head. She could see how crinkled and dried up he looked, how parched and weak he was.

So that's what she did. Holding on tightly to the conductor, she quickly reached out her other hand and took the little fellow and popped him into her jacket pocket. She zipped him up and grabbing hold of the rope with both hands she shouted to the others to haul her up.

Alex, Bea and Harry hauled and pulled, hand over hand. Sophia was quite heavy but they managed to heave her up the side of the box. Then she put a leg over the edge, and the other, and then jumped down, collapsing in the bottom of the box with a huge sigh of relief as she undid the rope.

'WELL? Soph, did you get him?' They eyed her up.

Slowly she opened her zip pocket, pulled the little fellow out and placed him sitting in the palm of her hand. Here he was at last. Very like his brother Ege, but looking tattered and torn with his wavy white hair all blown about, little raggedy jerkin of dark blue, and holey leggings. He had lost his hat.

'Oh, little Ogo Pogo, you looked wrecked!' said Alex.

'Water,' croaked the tiny wavering voice. 'Water, please!' Bea got the water bottle.

She wasn't sure how to give him the water, but she poured a little bit onto the corner of her skirt so that it was soaked. She screwed it into a little pointed shape, placed it carefully and gently against Ogo's minute mouth. It was hard to see exactly whether there was any water going in but there was a little sucking noise. As he sucked the moisture, he clearly began to revive, he started swelling a little, he looked less dehydrated and he opened his eyes wider. He kept sucking.

'Oh, that's better,' he whispered. 'Thank you so much everybody, thank you for saving me, all of you. I thought I was going to die out there!'

And the children smiled at each other. They were so proud of themselves for at last achieving the mission that they had set out to do.

'When you've rested a bit, Ogo, we will want to hear all about your adventure,' said Alex. 'But in the meantime, would you be happy to sleep in Sophia's zipped up pocket while we work out a way to get you home?'

'Absolutely NO problem!' squeaked Ogo. And after he had had another suck of Bea's damp skirt, Sophia gently placed him safely into her pocket and zipped it up.

Bea suddenly got the giggles. She realised it must look ridiculous holding up her damp skirt for little Ogo Pogo to suck. The whole idea was ludicrous. As she started giggling, Sophia felt overcome with relief and couldn't help chuckling too with Bea. And then it was just so infectious, all of them started giggling — and laughing. And soon all four of them were gasping for breath, hiccupping and coughing. They laughed and laughed until their sides ached and tears streamed down their faces.

And together they chanted the magic spell.

'Box! Take us back to the rib!' Alex laughed.

"Look, I'm good at this sort of thing. I do it at gymnastics,
and I'm not the least bit scared!" Sophia said.

Chapter 18

The box landed neatly on the shore by the rib and everyone wriggled out. Alex ran back to the lighthouse and carefully closed the door, making sure it locked again properly. He jogged back to the others with Bunty who had been patiently waiting for them all.

They were sitting cross-legged in a group looking at each other.

'What's up?' he asked.

'We are trying to work out what to do next,' replied Harry. 'Obviously, we must get the rib back to its mooring, Bunty back to Gar Gar, me back to Daddy and Mummy at Nacton House, Bea back to Uncle Tom and Auntie Dee Dee's house at Kettleburgh. Those are the places in the straightest line. But, and most importantly, we must get Pogo back to Parham as soon as we can. Quite a lot still to do! And we're not sure in what order to do what.'

'Well, let's have a drink of water and something to eat,' said Bea. She nipped to the rib and returned with an apple each and the water bottle. 'Good thing there's still some food left,' she remarked. Bunty eyed up the apples, looking very hungry. 'I expect she's thirsty too after swallowing all that salty sea water.'

Sophia poured a little water from the bottle into Bea's cupped hands and Bunty licked and licked them.

'Ew!' exclaimed Bea, 'Very tickly!' And she bit off a piece of her apple and gave it to Bunty. 'There you go girl,' she said kindly.

Alex took charge, looking at his watch. 'Right, well, it's now getting on for 4pm and we've still got a couple of hours till dark. We should get Bunty home in time for her supper by 5pm if possible, and once she's safely back with Gar Gar, that will make everything else easier too.'

'Let's just focus for a minute and see what we come up with.'

So the four of them sat in their circle cross-legged and held hands. They were getting used to doing this ESP thing and quite liked it. It was still peaceful and calm out at sea and they felt relaxed.

'I think this is what we should do,' said Harry after a while. 'I think Alex, and maybe me, should motor the rib back to its mooring while Sophia and Bea and Bunty go in the magic box back to Garg's house. Then, those two could come back to the mooring and collect Alex and me and then we all fly back to Nacton.'

'Oooer...' said Sophia, 'I'm worried about Alex driving the rib back through those choppy waters and channels of shingle again.'

'Yes, but Sophia, the tide will have turned by now. It will be taking us INTO the river, not out of it, and will be higher than it was. Also, the wind has dropped and any there is, will be behind us. I really think it will be 'plain sailing'!' Alex replied, smiling. 'I think it's a good plan Harry, and I could do with some company on the way back. I guess we'd rather Sophia went in the box to make sure Ogo is really safe, but Harry, why don't you go with Sophia and Bunty, and Bea can come with me? I think you deserve a break in guaranteed dry conditions (hopefully)! You can explain something to Gar Gar — though what on earth you'll say, heaven only knows!'

'Don't worry about that, Alex. You leave that to us, we'll think of something, won't we, Sophia?' replied Harry.

So, with that, the four of them assembled on the beach. Sophia and Harry turned the box on its side and tying Bunty round the middle with the rope again, managed to lure her into the box by offering her a cheese sandwich. Then, and although Bunty wasn't too happy about this, they manoeuvred the box so that it was upright again, with her inside. Sophia and Harry scrambled up the side of the rib and one by one jumped into the bottom of the box next to Bunty who was looking a little confused and restless.

'Bunty, SIT!' said Sophia with authority. And Bunty sat down obediently and the two children sat in the bottom of the box. They loudly chanted the magic words, adding, 'Take us to Gar Gar's house,' and the box immediately disappeared from view.

Alex gave a little involuntary shiver. 'Oh, golly, I just hope they'll be ok,' he murmured.

Next Alex and Bea climbed aboard the rib, straightened everything out and starting the engine, they turned it southwards, and began motoring along the coast back down to the mouth of the river.

Beatrix glanced backwards. *What a lighthouse!* she thought. *It's an amazing building and I really hope someone saves it from falling into the sea very soon.*

Chapter 19

While Alex and Bea motored up the coast, the
magic box swung into Gar Gar's back garden and
neatly landed. Sophia and Harry had instructed it
to land right behind the compost heaps out of
sight, and the two of them and Bunty scrambled
out.

'Ouch – blinking nettles!' exclaimed Sophia.
Bunty had already pelted up the garden to the
open French doors. The two children sprinted
behind her. They slowed down and sauntered into
the sunny dining room trying to look relaxed. Gar
Gar was in her study in a paint spattered apron,
her hair all over the place, half up half down –
large paintbrush between her teeth, glasses on the
end of her nose. She looked a little bit like
something between a pirate and a gypsy. She was
eyeing up one of her huge canvasses on her easel.
It was a painting of a vast ocean – all stormy and
grey.

'Wow! That's realistic, Gargs!' said Harry
with feeling.

She launched into a plethora of statements
and questions – 'Oh hello you two little darlings!
Where did you spring from? How lovely to see you!
Thanks for bringing Bunty back. I hope she's been
a good girl and wasn't a nuisance for everyone?
Did you have a good picnic? I hope she didn't get
at everyone's food? Did she get enough exercise
do you think, or should I take her for a run before
her supper?'

Sophia wasn't sure where to begin. 'Er... well, Gargs, I think Bunty's probably had enough exercise for today. She did lots of... er... swimming and running about, didn't she Harry?'

'Yes Gargs, she has, and she's been really well behaved too!' added Harry.

'Really?' replied Gar Gar laughing. 'That's rare! Please would you give her her supper? She can have it now, while I make you a drink and snack. By the way, how did you get here? Where are Mummy and Daddy? Are they all coming for a cuppa too?' And she filled up the kettle and switched it on anyway.

Sophia and Harry measured out Bunty's food and added the water with a bit extra for good measure. Bunty hoovered the food up as if she had never eaten before.

'Wow, well, she's certainly hungry!' observed Gar Gar. And with that, Bunty went off into the dining room and collapsed under the table, in total exhaustion.

Bearing a tray with cups of milk and cheesy oat biscuits into the sunlit dining room, Gar Gar sat down with her cup of tea, and ushered the children in to join her. They sat at her brightly patterned table cloth and started gobbling up the snacks almost as quickly as Bunty had.

'Now then, you'd better tell me all about your afternoon. I can tell something fishy has been going on, you two! Tell me everything... AND where the others are!' she added.

Sophia and Harry looked at each other sheepishly. Then with a little nod they started the story.

Omitting anything connected with near drownings and being dangled in space 30 metres above the ground, the two children told Gar Gar nearly everything.

'So, you see, Gargs, we need to get back to Alex and Bea, on the rib, that they've got onto the mooring by now, hopefully,' Sophia concluded.

'Well, wow, that is quite a story!' exclaimed Gar Gar. 'But I have to say, I'm not a bit surprised. Ogo Pogo and Ege Pege always were up for adventures — and mischief too. I'm just SO glad you found Ogo. It would, as Tom and Joe said, have been a complete disaster if he had got lost. It's a very good thing Rose didn't know about all this. Congratulations children, you've all been very brave and very clever and I'm proud of you!'

'Do you want to see him, Gargs?' asked Sophia. And she unzipped her jacket pocket and opened it up. Gar Gar peered into the dark pocket and could just make out a little sleeping fellow. Tiny squeaky snores came from him. 'I think best to just zip that little chap safely up, snuggle him back in there and keep your jacket on you,' she said, adding: 'There's only one thing I'm a bit worried about. It's already nearly five p.m and it will be dark in an hour or so. I don't quite understand the 'time' thing. I'm hoping Tom's experiment means you will get back to Nacton, Kettleburgh and Parham at around the time you left, but in any case I'm going to give you a torch and some more snacks for the others. You never know, you might need them.' And she went and got the torch that Jon had given to Gar Gar's husband Jos for Christmas. 'Bring it back sometime won't you, or I'll be in trouble! Good thing Jos is out at the golf club. Now do take me down the garden and show me your magic box.'

Bunty was too tired to move as the three of them made their way down the garden.

'Gosh! Well, it's just a big cardboard box really, isn't it?' said Gar Gar. 'Nothing really special, and yet... and yet... Well, wow... it really is an extraordinary bit of magic! And all you do is say the words of the chant?'

'Well, Ege said he put in a little extra magic too,' said Sophia.

'Oh did he? That's strange. I didn't think Ogo and Ege had much in the way of magic powers of their own, actually. Usually, they used to get extra magical help - spells and what not — from 'Magic Joe' who used to live in the woods at Redgrave in the old days. But I've no idea where he lives now. Hmm I wonder...?'

And Gar Gar seemed to go off into a world of her own for a minute, but then quickly snapped back to attention. 'Right, come on Harry and Soph! Let's get you going and back to Alex and Bea. Take care of yourselves, won't you - and of little Ogo Pogo. Be strong - keep your heads up. Love you!'

'Love you too, Gargs!' And with that the children wriggled into the box, and Gar Gar heard the chant:

'We play in the box,
We play in the box,
We play in the box,
All day!
Take us back to Alex and Bea at the rib!'

Next thing she knew, the box had disappeared out of sight.

She picked a few handfuls of parsley from the vegetable patch and, distracted by her thoughts, absent-mindedly made her way up the garden back to the house.

There was a beautiful sky to the west.

Chapter 20

Meanwhile, back on the river, Alex and Bea were making good progress in the rib. They had motored without event down the coast of Shingle Street to the mouth of the river. The tide and breeze took them into the river without any problems. This time Alex had managed to navigate the channels successfully. Bea was helpful, giving Alex confidence. As they motored through the deep-water channels, she said 'well done Alex!' in all the right places. From then on, Alex sped up river to Orford, chugged through the moorings and then full pelt again up river from Orford to Aldeburgh.

There was a beautiful blue, pink and purple sky to the West as they approached the yacht club. Even from a distance, Alex and Bea could plainly see quite a crowd of people outside the Club House having tea and drinks as they admired the view. The remarkable sunsets, not surprisingly, were popular with the sailors where they could enjoy their 'sundowners'.

'Bother!' said Alex 'The tide is still quite low. I daren't motor as close as I would like to the far bank. In addition, all the racing has finished and there are no other boats about. We're going to stand out terribly!'

'Hmmm,' replied Bea. 'What do you think we should do Alex? Sit up as tall as we can, look as big as possible and hope that we don't get noticed?'

By now they were approaching East Bank buoy, parallel with the Martello Tower. It wouldn't be long before they would have to cruise past the Club House with all those adults ready to bellow at them.

Alex cut the engine. No one at the Club House had seen the approaching rib yet. He sat there for a bit thinking what to do. He looked around him, taking in the scene. Up ahead, to starboard, on the river shore, peaceful in the late afternoon sun, was the little shell beach, and further up from there, the old rubbish tip. Behind him along the shore down towards Martello, nothing but mud. Nowhere to land. He knew he could never beach the rib along here, no way! To the port side, the river was beginning to fill up, but had a way to go. There was not much except a few moorings and river marker buoys.

Bea followed his gaze. 'Am I thinking what you're thinking Alex?' she asked, adding, 'I'm thinking we should pick up one of those boat moorings a little further back down the river towards Half Way point, and just tie up there and wait for the others. I honestly think it would be madness to try and bluff our way past the Club House. Look! It's teeming with grownups.'

'True fact Bea! I agree – let's do that,' replied Alex 'I was just thinking about Soph and Harry. They'll find us, won't they? All they have to do is instruct the box to come back to the rib and it will — wherever we are.'

So that's what they did. They motored a little way back down the river and as they turned into the tide, Bea leaned over the edge and caught one of the spare boat moorings on the far side of the river. She clung onto it with all her strength as Alex turned off the engine and came to the bow. He helped Bea tie the buoy to the rib's painter. They sat back in the rib surrounded by pink and turquoise blue tinted sky and prepared to wait for Sophia and Harry. 'I'm sure they won't be too long,' said Alex reassuringly.

He busied himself tidying up the rib just as he'd seen Jon doing countless times. He picked up the extra borrowed jackets and lifejackets. He coiled the ropes, wiped the seats with the old towel and folded that up too. He put away the kill chord and stowed the ignition key safely back in its box under the wheel. Sweeping up the crumbs and wrappers from the floor, he knew he would have some explaining to do to his Daddy, as to why the rib wasn't on its correct mooring. He would also have to explain away the lifejackets, not to mention the pair of binoculars. He wasn't looking forward to any of that; no, not one bit.

'I'd be interested to know what happened to the rest of your Lego aeroplane, Alex,' remarked Bea after a bit. 'I never saw any of it even though we went over the lighthouse area very carefully.'

'I know' replied Alex, 'I've wondered that too. Ogo Pogo will have a lot to tell us when he's fully recovered, won't he!'

And just as he finished his sentence, as if on cue, there was a sudden 'WHOOSH', and a large cardboard box landed just behind the driving seat.

'Aargh! Bumpy landing!' Giggling could be heard coming from inside it, and Alex and Bea started laughing with relief. 'Here they are!'

Sophia and Harry extracted themselves from the box and the two of them briefly told Alex and Bea about their successful interview with Gar Gar.

'And Ogo Pogo's still safely crashed out in my pocket,' concluded Sophia, laughing. 'He snores, by the way!' and they all thought that was very funny.

They were all relieved to see each other again and to know that this part of their mission had gone smoothly at least. Alex and Bea got lots of praise from Sophia and Harry for their safe navigation of the rib and clever decision about tying it up to a spare mooring. 'Good plan, Alex and Bea!' said Harry.

So, without wasting too much time in discussion, the children all got back into the box, with the binoculars, the rope and the spare jackets. They decided they might as well take the lifejackets as well, for extra padding to sit on. They knew they would have to return them to the club's lost property box pretty soon. But just not today. They began to feel as if the box had become rather a comfortable home. Chanting the magic words, they instructed the magic box to take them back to Nacton. Alex for one, peering down his straw, was not sorry to see the rib disappear way below them as the box climbed up into the sky and flew over the top of the Club House and headed south with the river and sea far beneath them.

'We've got some more provisions from Gargs,' said Soph. 'We already had a snack with her, but would you like some?'

'Are you kidding? We're starving!' exclaimed Bea and Alex in unison. So, Sophia gave out some of the oatcakes and cheese and some drinks of oat milk which Gar Gar had put in water bottles. There were some carrot sticks too. 'Yummy!' they said.

The magic box flew on in land for a while as the four of them looked through their little straw periscopes and tried to work out where they were. They had passed over Snape Maltings and were heading inland now. It was a beautiful golden early evening. The last rays of sun were still glowing in a golden and orange sky. There were woods and trees below them.

But then, just as the children were beginning to feel relaxed and confident, something simply beastly happened.

Chapter 21

The magic box started juddering and stuttering as if it had a cough. It was losing speed and beginning to descend in swoops and jolts down towards the ground. It was heading straight for some trees.

'What's going on?' cried Harry and Bea. 'Why's the box doing that?'

'I don't know!' shouted Alex.

'Let's try doing the chant again!' cried Sophia.

So they tried the magic chant again in loud voices, careful to stay in unison.

'It's NOT responding!' cried Harry in distress. 'We're still going down!'

And sure enough, the box was still going downwards and the ground was approaching more rapidly than they liked the look of.

'Quick, grab the lifejackets and put them around you and under you!' shouted Alex. 'Sophia, make sure you put some padding round your pocket where Ogo is.'

'Oh, don't be so bossy, Alex,' said Sophia irritably, 'I'm not stupid,' as she carefully lay curled up on a lifejacket with her jacket pocket nicely cocooned in a wodge of thick material.

The magic box came to a shuddering halt and fell with a bump to the ground. It rolled onto its side.

'Oh my God!' said Sophia grumpily. 'This is really annoying,' she added, as she crawled out of the box. 'Here we are in the middle of a blinking wood in the middle of blinking nowhere.'

The other three crawled out and brushed themselves down, looking around.

'Well, at least we aren't hurt, Soph,' said Bea.

With that there was a little squeaky shout coming from Sophia's jacket pocket. 'Let me out!' came a tiny squawk. She gingerly opened it and pulled out little Ogo Pogo and placed him on her open hand.

'I'm afraid it's my fault that the magic box has come down here. You see, I wanted it to.'

'What?' they gasped. 'Why?'

'Before I tell you the whole story children,' Ogo squeaked, 'I think we should set up camp here. We need a small fire to keep us warm, but also for another reason which I will explain to you later. I wonder if we could make one. Hmmm, let me see, what we need is some dry kindling and bits and pieces and a small fire circle, just here.' Sophia placed Ogo carefully down on a nearby tree stump.

They were in a little clearing in the middle of the woods. The last rays of warm sunlight were falling directly onto a patch of shrubby ground where they were standing. Bea and Sophia went to collect some small pieces of coarse bark, tinder wood, dried grass, and dry leaves. Harry started making a circle clearing with a stick. Ogo Pogo was looking at Alex.

'Alex,' he squeakily whispered, 'have you got any matches?'

'No,' he replied. 'One thing I think we could do is that thing with a wooden stick in another piece of wood, rubbing it in circles quickly to make it hot, like Bear Grylls did on TV. But that could take forever.'

And then Alex had a flash of inspiration. Drawing Joe's old Swiss army knife out of his pocket, he opened it up and splayed out the gadgets. There amongst them was what he was looking for... the magnifying glass.

Harry shredded some of the driest pieces of grass and kindling carefully in the little fire circle as the last bright ray of sunshine fell directly onto it. Alex held the magnifying glass steadily on top of the kindling so that the sunlight was directly going through it. The magnifying glass created a small intense bright dot on the dry tinder where the sun shone through it. They watched and waited.

After about 5 minutes a little trail of smoke appeared under the magnifying glass. Soon there was a flame and the little pieces of dry grasses began to burn. Alex drew back the glass and Harry blew gently at the bottom of the little fire, slowly adding tiny pieces of tinder.

'Wow! That's so cool!' Bea said admiringly.

'Right, now then children,' said Ogo, sitting up on the tree stump right next to them, 'you sit down — keep feeding the fire Harry — and I'll explain what's going on.'

The children sat round the little fire and settled down. There was a magical dusky light in the woodland as the golden sun began to sink at last behind the trees. The sky became all colours of reds and streaky orange. At last the children were going to hear Ogo Pogo's story.

'Firstly,' he squeaked, 'I need to say a proper thank you for coming to rescue me. I realise I've caused quite a bit of trouble. And I am most grateful to you all. It's true that I always wanted to fly. I always wanted to go and visit my relations in New Zealand, but now I know that is a long way away. It was a silly thing to fly out of your window Alex, on your Lego aeroplane, but I got a chance, and... well, I took it! I wanted first to go and find Magic Joe. You see I haven't seen him for so long. I thought he might help me fly further with his magic. So I flew to Redgrave woods where he used to live. But when I got there, Blackie the old blackbird told me that he had moved to some woods near the coast, near a village called Blaxhall. I really do want to see Magic Joe again. And, well, here we are. I'm afraid I put a little curse on your magic spell to take us to Nacton. While you were saying your spell, I whispered, "Stop at Blaxhall woods on the way," though of course, you didn't hear me. The box had received mixed messages, and that's why it came to land here.'

'But what happened when you first flew the plane?' asked Sophia respectfully. 'How did you get caught up on Orford lighthouse, Ogo?'

'It was the wind that took me off course, actually. You know it was quite breezy and I couldn't control the plane. Then I found I was being blown always northwards and overshot this wood. I was heading out to sea really rapidly. I couldn't land, I couldn't stop. I saw the lighthouse ahead and thought maybe, just maybe, I could catch hold of it to stop myself from drowning in those massive waves ahead. I was really scared, I can tell you. The aeroplane smashed into that bit of metal at the side of the lighthouse and I clung on to it. I don't think I could have held on much longer. The plane just shot off into the sea and was washed away, leaving just the nose of the plane, which fell down near the base of the lighthouse. I'm very sorry I lost your Lego plane, Alex.'

'But that red Lego nose tip, that was my clue!' said Harry proudly.

'You all did really well,' carried on Ogo Pogo. 'Discovering the clues, finding them and everything. It was brilliant to see you all. Honestly, I thought I would shrivel up completely and die.'

'Well, you're safe now,' said Sophia kindly.

Just then there was a scuffling sound in the woods behind them followed by the sound of little footsteps, snifflings and gruntings.

'What the — ?'

From behind a tree a small grey and brown spikey hedgehog, with a little black snout, shuffled into view. He paused and looked at the assembled company and then shuffled up nearer to them.

'Ah... there you are Ogo,' grunted the little creature in a snorty gruff little voice. We hoped we'd find you!'

'We?' asked Sophia curiously.

Alex beamed from ear to ear. He was particularly thrilled to see a real live talking hedgehog – it was one of his absolutely favourite animals.

And with that another little creature, about 20 centimetres tall, danced out from behind the tree. She was much, much bigger than the Ogo Pogo who looked tiny beside her. But she was much, much smaller than the children. She was a little pixie-like character with a mop of golden curls and an impish grin, and pointy ears. Dressed in brown leaves, a little skirt of tawny flowers, and a green mossy cap on her head, she carried a little woven basket. Wearing a shoulder bag made of green leaves, she he was bare-footed and rather raggedy. She had a big smile and rosy cheeks.

'Hedgy!' she cried, 'Oh! I see you found Ogo and his friends! Well done, you!' and she clapped her hands with excitement.

Magic Merry danced out from behind the tree

Chapter 22

The children were stunned into silence. They had never seen a talking hedgehog or a little creature like HER before!

'Ogo Pogo! How are you?!' exclaimed the little pixie girl excitedly in her high-pitched voice.

'But, wait a minute,' squeaked Ogo. 'Who the...? Well, I'm fine now, thanks to these friends of mine. Let me introduce you. Alex, Sophia, Harry, Bea, this is... this is... er... so sorry, but I don't know your name. You are very like Magic Joe to look at... but...'

'Oh! Didn't you know? I'm Magic Merry. Well, my real name's Mary, but everyone calls me Merry, and this is my dear hedgehog friend, Hedgy. I'm Magic Joe's twin sister. We've been waiting for you to arrive. I hoped you'd light a little fire so that I could find you!' Gosh, Merry could talk so quickly!

'Well, I suggested lighting it partly for that very reason,' replied Ogo.

Everybody gasped. 'Wow!' they said in unison.

Merry was so very, well... merry! She was full of smiles, with bright laughter in her eyes. She was so friendly and happy, it was contagious; the children immediately felt happy too. They listened intently to what she was saying.

'But how did you know I was coming?' asked Ogo Pogo.

'A seagull told me,' replied Merry. 'He flew over early this morning and said you were looking for my brother, Magic Joe, and that you'd been to Redgrave woods. A blackbird told the seagull. You know what a lot of gossips there are around! So, I worked out you would come this way next. Oh Hedgy!' she suddenly interrupted herself, 'would you mind awfully, be a pet, and go to my house and collect some peppermint leaves and that acorn cake, and we'll make some tea – oh and you'll need a kettle and some cups.' Hedgy snuffled in agreement and then, borrowing Merry's basket, shuffled off into the woods.

Then Merry continued explaining: 'I heard you were looking for Magic Joe, but the trouble is, he's gone to look for YOU!'

'Excuse me Merry,' interrupted Bea politely, 'but how old are you exactly? If you don't mind me asking.'

'Oh! I couldn't possibly tell you. I NEVER tell anyone my age,' said Merry, laughing. 'In fact, I can't really remember. But one thing, you see, because we are magic, little folk like me are much older than we ever look! Now look here, Ogo Pogo, what exactly did you want Magic Joe for? Is there anything I can do to help?'

'Well,' squeaked Ogo. There were two things really. One thing was that I had a chance in that aeroplane to go and find Magic Joe again. I haven't seen him for SO long. Also, once I'd found him, I thought he might help me with some magic to make me fly further. Even all the way to New

Zealand. But I had a terrible crash and ended up stranded at the top of Orford lighthouse. Merry, it was like being on the edge of a huge world. A vast world that scared me rather. If it wasn't for these children, I think something dreadful might have happened to me there. After such a danger I feel the need to see Magic Joe even more, but I definitely never want to go to New Zealand!'

'Well,' said Merry brightly, 'Just thank goodness you are OK, Ogo. It would have been terrible for everybody if you had got lost at sea.'

'YES!' chorused the children with feeling (though no-one more so than Harry!).

'Tears welled up in Ogo's eyes. 'I'm so very sorry for all the trouble I caused.'

'Oh, don't worry Ogo Pogo,' said Alex soothingly, 'we've had just the most wonderful adventure – haven't we everyone?' and the other children nodded vigorously. Harry gave a little wink to the others.

Just then a bright little animal scampered into view. It was a little brown field mouse with a twitchy pointed snout, small rounded ears, a long tail, and whiskers. He was dragging something behind him.

'Oh hello, Nibbler!' exclaimed Merry. 'How lovely to see you this evening. These are my new friends: Alex, Sophia, Harry and Bea. Would you like to join us?' The children's eyes looked like they were going to pop out of their heads in surprise. *Whatever next?* they thought.

'Well, yes I would!' the little mouse squealed. 'Hedgy asked me to bring these things to you and he's coming along in a minute... but you know how slow he is!'

And the field mouse put down some tiny acorn cups round the fire. Harry put a few extra small pieces of wood on it to get it going, and soon Hedgy shuffled back to the group, bringing the kettle and a little round cake on a piece of bark as a tray.

It was a jolly tea party. Alex collected the extra leftover snacks from the magic box and put them out to share. The children sat in a circle with Merry, Ogo Pogo, Hedgy and Nibbler. They drank peppermint tea from acorn cups, and ate tiny slices of nutty tasting cake. Everyone was laughing, it was such a happy time. Merry told them stories of good fairies and naughty goblins, helpful brownies and brave elves. She talked about her happy childhood with her twin brother Magic Joe.

It was a time that the four children would remember for the rest of their lives — tea with that strange little collection of creatures. The darkening woods felt mellow, mysterious and alive in the warm gloaming. The branches of the trees wrapped themselves around the little group and the children felt safe and secure. A few stars began to glow, and way up in the indigo sky, a sliver of silver moon appeared above the tree tops. Merry got a little fiddle and wooden whistle from out from the bottom of her shoulder bag. She played them some jigs and reels. Hedgy played on the wooden whistle and joined in with the reels. The four children tapped their feet and then jumped up and started dancing around the glowing sparkling fire.

As darkness fell the pretty calling birds came down to roost in the branches of the trees all around them. Soon everybody felt sleepy. The four children felt so contented, so tired, so happy and relaxed. Using the torch, they made a camp, spread out the lifejackets round the fireplace and curled up under the other jackets next to each other. The embers from the fire created a warm glow. All was quiet apart from the hooting of the wise old owl, and a few little snaps and crackles of twigs, as little creatures sneaked back into their night nests and homes. Ogo was safely zipped up into Sophia's pocket, gently snoring again. Merry, Hedgy and Nibbler crept away back to their own little dwellings under the oak tree. A nightingale began singing in the distance.

Alex, Sophia, Harry and Bea lay on their backs gazing up at the clear starry sky. Bea shone her torch around the trees and Alex tried to peer at the constellations through his rather small magnifying glass.

'We really have had the most exciting day, haven't we!' said Bea. 'What a lot we did! I think we did really well! What a team!'

'It was awesome,' agreed Sophia. She and Bea would have liked to chat about everything that happened all over again.

But Harry was intrigued by the sky. He said 'Bea can you turn that torch off a minute? If we look carefully, we might get to see some of the constellations. You know, groups of stars that make shapes and are called things.'

'Yes, look! There's one,' replied Alex. 'That one over there, that looks like a saucepan with a handle. It's actually called the Ursa Minor which means 'Small Bear' in some other language or other.'

'Oh, that's Latin,' said Harry. 'Yes! Look! The saucepan's handle bit is actually the Little Bear's tail and he has a square body and four short legs!'

'Cool!' Bea said yawning.

'Ahhhh, now you made me yawn, Bea!' said Sophia, yawning too, and as she slowly dozed off, she muttered... 'Yes, and at the end of the Small Bear's tail is a very bright star — the brightest we have — called the North Star...' And her voice trailed off.

All four children soon drifted into a deep sleep. Their dreams were of glowing woodland glades, leaves falling like golden coins, carpets of white spring snowdrops and bright yellow aconites. They dreamed of tiny smiling spikey creatures with long turquoise tails. They dreamed of green-eyed little ancient men, of Magic Merry and Magic Joe waving sparklers. They dreamed of their dear homes, of their sweet sisters Bella and Ellie, and of their very own warm beds, quiet and safe.

Chapter 23

Early next morning as dawn approached, Bea woke up first. It was twilight. The birds were twittering away for their dawn chorus. It was a beautiful sound and Bea marvelled at it. However, it was gloomy in the wood, and, shivering, Bea felt rather cheerless and chilly. She pulled her jacket around her a bit closer. She was beginning to feel hungry and missing her Mummy, Daddy and Bella. She was a teeny bit homesick.

She nudged Alex. 'Wake up, Alex,' she whispered. Alex stirred but did not wake up. Bea peered at Alex's watch. 6am — still pretty early. Crawling off her lifejacket, Bea squatted down by the fire and poked it with a stick. Not much action there. Just a few embers but mostly warm ash. She wondered what she could do. She was beginning to long for them all to wake up and get going. She knew she couldn't get the fire to start and in addition she had this growing sensation that something was going on at home — that she needed to be there. *That might be my sixth sense,* she said to herself... I wonder... what shall I do?'

Bea sauntered off in the direction of the trees. She kicked and shuffled through the leaves discontentedly. She began to feel uneasy — a real urgency to get away from this place.

She started calling quietly, 'Merry! Merry! Are you there, please can you wake up? Merry, Hedgy... anyone?'

'Shhhh! came a high-pitched voice from within the roots of the trees. It was Nibbler. His whiskers were twitching and he looked sleepy. 'What's all this noise about Bea? Everyone's still asleep.'

'I know,' said Bea, 'I'm so sorry, but I have a bad feeling this morning and wanted to see Merry – I wanted to talk to her.'

'Well OK, Bea, just follow me, and I'll take you to her,' said Nibbler kindly. Bea was led away by the scampering field mouse and his long tail. They ducked under some trees and then to Bea's surprise, Nibbler started dashing up one of the trees which was full of branches. 'Come on then, Bea!' whispered Nibbler.

Bea, found to her amazement, that the branches of the tree were easy to climb. Bea was good at gymnastics and her legs were very bendy. She could easily stretch and reach each branch, hand over hand, foot after foot — it was like a climbing frame. The branches seemed to present themselves magically to her just at the right moment. *Wow this is cool!* she thought. Up and up they climbed until they were nearly at the top of the tree.

The tree canopy suddenly cleared, and there, nestling in amongst the top branches, protected by the top layer of leaves, was the most wonderful little tree house Bea had ever seen. It was about the size of Bella's favourite Sylvania toy house. Sitting on a wooden platform between three branches, there was a roofed cabin, with a chimney and little curtained windows. The cabin was made of pieces of overlapping bark, the roof of packed moss and grass. Smoke was curling from the little chimney. There was a tree swing. There was a pulley system for Merry's basket which was next to a slide that went down the back of the tree. All around were nesting birds, chattering and calling to one another. The sun was coming up and the whole scene was bathed in early morning sunlight.

Bea gasped and wedged herself in the nearest forked branch to admire the little house. 'Wow,' she thought, 'I wish Daddy would build us a tree house like this!'

Nibbler politely knocked at the door and quite quickly it opened wide and there was a beaming Magic Merry. He explained to her that Bea wanted to talk to her.

'Oh, good morning Bea! How lovely to see you. Quite bright and early. I was just brewing up some nettle tea. Would you like some?'

'Yes please,' replied Bea politely. 'I'm very sorry to trouble you so early in the day. I just had an overwhelming feeling that I needed to talk to you, Merry. I've got such a funny feeling inside my tummy. It's as if something is happening at home and I don't know what it is.'

'Well! We should always listen to our feelings and try and work out what they are telling us!' replied Merry sympathetically. She popped inside and came back with two walnut shell cups of tea. Bea sipped hers, trying to make it last — it was such a tiny amount! 'Now then, tell me,' Merry encouraged her.

'Well,' said Bea, 'it's as if something is happening with my sister, Bella. You know she is nearly five and is at Joe's house playing with Ellie, Harry's sister. We left them there when we went to try and find Ogo Pogo in the magic flying box. I'm not sure if Bella is in danger but there is something happening, and I want to be there to make sure she's alright, or Ellie is, or something. I feel like we need to go quite soon and quickly.' Bea's eyes filled up.

Magic Merry sat next to Bea on the little platform and stroked Bea's hand with her tiny one.

'Well Bea, as I said, we should always listen to our feelings and let them speak to us. Sometimes we feel things quite strongly and they aren't always there for the right reasons. Sometimes our feelings or emotions can be a result of tiredness, hunger, happy or sad events. We just have to be quiet sometimes to try and work out which feelings are telling us something useful and which are just a reaction. Hmmm. Let's close our eyes and take a moment to ourselves.'

So, Bea and Merry closed their eyes. Bea could hear the pretty twittering of the birds in the woodland. She listened to the 'tuk tuk' of a woodpecker in the distance and a bee buzzing quite close to her right ear. There was a smell of fragrant flowers and the fresh air of an early summer's morning. The taste of nettle tea was pleasant on her tongue. A shaft of sunlight landed on her and a pool of warmth spread into her, unwinding her body, her bones. She began to relax. In the palm of her hand she could feel the lightness of Merry's little hand resting there, and she felt a gentle tingling sensation emanating from it. It seemed to spread up Bea's arms and right through her. She was more contented than she had felt for ages. After a while she blinked open her eyes and could see little Merry looking at her with her twinkling and smiling eyes.

'How do you feel now Bea?'

'SO much better!' replied Bea in a whisper. 'That was, that was, well, you're simply magic, Merry!'

'Not completely Bea, you made that happen just as much as me. We just need time to slow down and stop sometimes, do a little of what you humans call 'meditation'! Now, what about your sixth sense, Bea, what is it telling you about Bella and Ellie now?'

'Well, I definitely don't feel so worried now. But I still feel we should all get going and get back to Nacton.'

'Right, well, that's what you'll do then. And MY sixth sense is telling me that this 'something' is connected with my naughty brother, Magic Joe. Who knows what tricks he might be up to?'

'Oh crumbs, I hadn't thought of that!' exclaimed Bea 'YES! That well might be IT!'

With that, Merry slid with a whoosh down her little slide, Bea clambered back down the branches of the wonderful tree and they made their way hurriedly back to the others. By now Alex, Sophia and Harry had just woken up, and were rubbing their eyes sleepily, looking around for Bea.

'Here I am!' said Bea, 'and here's Merry come to say goodbye to us. It's time to go!'

Without further explanations or ado, the four children drank some water, ate the last of the acorn cake, and tidied everything into the box. They cleared up round the little fireplace. Sophia checked that Ogo Pogo was still in her pocket and patted him gently… A muffled grumpy 'Oy!' could be heard.

'Thank you SO much Merry,' said Bea, 'We love you,' and was going to try and hug her but wasn't quite sure how to go about it, without squashing her!

Hedgy and Nibbler had shuffled and scampered down to the little camp to wave goodbye.

'Yes, thank you, Merry! We've had a wonderful time!' chorused all the other children. 'Thank you Hedgy! Thank you, Nibbler!' And they blew kisses at them all as they piled and wriggled into the box.

Merry pulled a little wooden wand from out of her shoulder bag. It had strange carved markings on it. Holding it up above the box she circled the wand three times in each direction and called in a strong voice:

'Box, box, fly with care,

Take them all directly there.
Earth below and sky above,
Fly away just like a dove.
The time has come, renewed by sun,
To count our blessings, one by one.
Take them to Joe's house, Nacton!'

And she called to the children, 'Use your own magic chant next time. The box will be fine again now! Byeeee!!'

And the box shot out of the woods up into the air.

"So much better!" replied Bea in a whisper.
"You're simply magic, Merry!"

Chapter 24

THE DAY BEFORE

It was just after lunch. Bella and Ellie were busy upstairs at Joe and Clare's house. They didn't even notice that the older cousins had disappeared – they were playing puppy dogs. This involved Ellie, in her Dalmatian dressing up onesie outfit, being led around the room on a lead by Bella. Bella enjoyed practising her commands such as 'sit', 'stay', 'walk', 'lie down'! They loved this game, taking it in turns. On other occasions Bella played it with Bea and sometimes one of them pretended to be a pony, on a lunge rope, being schooled by the other.

'Ellie, shall we go down into the garden and play the game there?' asked Bella 'We could play ball and I could throw it for you to fetch!?   You know that game. We play that with Bunty sometimes at Gar Gar's, don't we, but of course, Bunty is SO disobedient she won't drop the ball — she is such a naughty funny puppy.'

'I know!' replied Ellie laughing 'She is SO cheeky AND she pulls me over if I try and hold her on the lead. But I like the way her ears flap up and down when she runs, don't you?'

'She pulls me too! AND she tries to eat the lead up,' added Bella. 'Well, she actually did once!' she reminded Ellie.

'I know!' replied Ellie again. 'AND she always has to have treats to get her to come to me! She is

SO greedy, she'll eat anything – even whole rabbits,' she added.

'Ooh I know, she really is a naughty girl' declared Bella — 'I've even heard my Mummy call her a 'menace'. I'm not sure what that is, but I think it means something REALLY dreadful.'

'OOH! Didn't Alex have a bunny rabbit called Dennis the Menace?' asked Ellie 'did Bunty eat that bunny too?'

'Oh, I expect so,' replied Bella.

'Yes, but I do love her,' said Ellie protectively. 'And so does Harry, especially. He told me he sometimes misses her SO, SO much when he's at school.'

'Well Ellie, I miss her when I'm in Germany,' responded Bella fervently, who was feeling a bit left out on the 'missing Bunty' front.

And thus the conversation went on, round and round.

At last the two little ones had made it down stairs (Ellie crawled down them on her front) and then Bella led Ellie on all fours out of the kitchen French doors into the lovely sunny garden. The two young rescue cats, Domino and Tigger, did not look very impressed, and hid under the table as the girls went past.

'Having fun?!' called Clare from the kitchen sink.

'Woof! woof!' came the enthusiastic reply.

They found a tennis ball. 'I'll hide the ball while you count to 20, Ellie. Then you must go and sniff and seek it out, just like Bunty does. Ready? No peeking!'

Ellie counted to 20 with her eyes squeezed firmly shut. Bella shot off down the garden with the ball. She found a large pine tree at the bottom near the shrubbery and circled round the base of it looking for a good hiding place. At the back of the tree was a little hole going into the roots. She hid the ball just at the entrance to the hole and then belted back to Ellie just as Ellie reached 20.

'Coming — ready or not!' shouted Ellie and she opened her eyes and looked about her. Bella was standing next to her panting, slightly smiling.

Ellie set off down the garden on all fours. She could crawl quite rapidly, though she was getting sore knees, so she stood up and started running. She had no idea where to look. The garden was big and full of great hiding places. She approached the hen run, thinking she would look in the egg-laying boxes just in case. Carefully she unlatched the door to the run and nipped in quickly. She knew she would be in trouble if she let any of the chickens out.

Nope, nothing there.

Locking the hen run, she circled round through the shrubbery and looked behind the summerhouse.

Nope, nothing there.

She had a look round the pond. Eventually she went back to Bella...

'It's no good Bella, I can't find it!' she cried. 'I've looked everywhere!'

So, Bella kindly led Ellie right to the bottom of the garden and stopped at the huge old pine tree. 'I put it just here behind the tree trunk at the base by the hole into the roots.'

Peering round the back of the tree, both of them gave a startled scream at the extraordinary sight that met their eyes.

Chapter 25

There, sitting casually on top of the tennis ball, was a small, cheerful looking little pixie boy. He had a mass of sticky out black hair, brown sparkling eyes, funny pointy ears and a dirty face! Wearing a pair of rather tatty trousers made of laurel leaves and a jacket of woven grass, he carried a shoulder bag made from two leaves stitched together. He had turned up little shoes and was about 20 centimetres tall. With a big smile and a cheeky expression, he looked very relaxed, content and pleased with himself. He clapped his hands merrily when he saw the children.

'Shhh! It's OK, don't scream,' he giggled, 'it's only me!'

Bella and Ellie eyes opened wide with disbelief. They were really curious, surprised and just a teeny bit scared.

'But who are you?' asked Bella bravely. 'You weren't here a minute ago!'

'Well I was, actually! I was just down in a tunnel here, underneath the tree. I think it's a little den that belongs to one of my mice friends. How do you do,' said the smiling character. 'Let me introduce myself. I'm Magic Joe! And you are...?'

'Oh WOW!' exclaimed Bella and Ellie together in unison.

'Well, I'm Magic Joe's daughter you see — I'm Ellie... Well, not THE Magic Joe — that's you —

but, the other Magic Joe. He's my Daddy, you see, but YOU are the real Magic Joe, aren't you? And this is my cousin Bella. Her Daddy, Uncle Tom, knows about you too, and so does my Auntie Rose...' And Ellie trailed off — she was getting hopelessly tied up in knots.

'Oh, that's superbly explained,' replied Magic Joe. 'I'm so pleased to meet you both and to know who you are.'

'Well – continued Bella, 'I don't think you know the rest of it all. My sister Bea, Ellie's brother Harry, and our cousins Alex and Sophia have gone flying in a big magic box thingy to look for our friend Ogo Pogo. And... oh dear, it's an awful lot to explain... I'm not sure I can...' and Bella trailed off too.

But little Magic Joe just grinned at them with such a happy smiley grin that both Ellie and Bella started giggling and laughing. They stopped worrying and began to feel quite merry themselves.

'Ah,' said Magic Joe with a wink, 'Yes, exactly. I'm hoping that between us all, we will be able to find him. You see I'm looking for him too. My friend Ray, the seagull, told me that Ogo Pogo was looking for me. But I don't know where he is now, or why he was looking for me. He's been such a silly fellow disappearing off like that and getting everyone so worried. It could be a disaster, as he will get ill if he doesn't get back to his little matchbox house soon. I thought I'd have a good look around your garden. You haven't seen him, have you children?'

'Oh no! Magic Joe, I've just been everywhere in the garden, and I didn't see him,' said Ellie.

Magic Joe continued, 'Well, I think next, after here, I will need to go to your garden at Kettleburgh, Bella, and have a good look there. I expect there are lots of good hiding places there.'

'Can we help you, Magic Joe?' asked Ellie. 'Can we come with you and look for Ogo?'

'Oh yes!' added Bella. 'Please say we can come with you! I know all the hiding places there and we could help you look. Ellie has such sharp eyes and could be very helpful too! Only one thing... how will we get there?' she asked curiously. 'I don't really want to go in that big box thing again. I didn't like being in there too much.'

Magic Joe stroked his chin for a minute thinking. 'Hmmm,' he said, 'I think it would be absolutely splendid if you two come and help me. But we mustn't upset Clare and Joe. I think if we leave a note pinned to this tree, when they come to look for you, they will find it and understand. Can you write, Bella?'

'Well, I'm not too bad at it,' replied Bella, 'I could try.'

'I can write!' cried Ellie, 'And I've got some pens and paper in the summer house.' And so Ellie ran up the garden and collected a large piece of paper and a fat felt-tipped pen. It was true that at the age of nearly four she COULD write!

With Bella's help she wrote:

Bella and me ave gon to
Tom hooz. We ar wiv majic Joe.
don wurry.
Ellie & Bella

And they pinned it to the tree with a drawing pin, as high up as they could manage.

Hopping up and down on one foot, Bella couldn't contain her excitement and asked yet again... 'But Magic Joe how exactly ARE we going to get there?'

Magic Joe gave the girls an enormous grin as he gently pulled a wooden carved stick, out of his shoulder bag. He whistled a low whistle and then said in a high clear voice:

'Friends on the earth,
Friends of the sky,
Come to us and help us fly.'

And he circled his stick three times in each direction.

Chapter 26

Two enormous Canada geese made graceful landings behind the fir tree at the bottom of the garden. With their huge wing spans and webbed feet splayed out in front of them, their arrival was thrilling to the little girls. Each one had glossy brown plumage, with a black head and neck, white splodge under their chins, black beak, white cheeks, and bright intelligent eyes.

The geese greeted Magic Joe enthusiastically. They adored him for all the kind things he had done for them over the years. They circled around him wagging their tail feathers and he stroked and patted them. They were very polite and helpful about carrying the small children to Kettleburgh. 'No problem at all, Magic Joe. We'd do anything for you!' they honked in their goosy voices.

'What?!' exclaimed Bella and Ellie together. 'Are we going to fly in the sky like real birds?' asked Ellie enthusiastically.

Magic Joe nodded and introduced the children to the two geese. Their names were Alberta and Nova. As Bella and Ellie climbed up onto their backs, they found the birds were soft to sit on. They had a little halter each to hold onto as well as the birds' necks and shoulders to put their arms around. They tucked their little feet just in front of the wings of each goose and both felt safe and secure.

Magic Joe reached up on tip toes and put the pen and some extra drawing paper in Ellie's pocket. 'You never know, we might need these!' he said.

Alberta looked round at Bella and gave her a little wink, which made Bella giggle.

A huge white herring seagull landed next to the geese. 'Ah good! There you are, Ray. I was just wondering where you had got to! Thanks so much for coming,' said Magic Joe. Ray was large and white, with grey wings and black markings on his head. He was quite stout, with a longish yellow bill, yellow legs and webbed feet. The girls thought he was terribly handsome. After a lot of patting and greetings, Magic Joe jumped up and sat astride Ray. 'Right! Hold tight and off we go!'

Ellie's Daddy, Joe, was hoeing the vegetable garden ready to plant his next crop of salad seeds. He and Clare loved growing vegetables and Joe was happiest on a Saturday when he could peacefully get on with a garden project. Gradually he became aware that it had grown rather quiet. He had had one eye on the little cousins and had got used to the noise of their woofing, calling to one another and counting. It slowly dawned on him that all he could hear was the sound of his hens clucking, sparrows, robins and blackbirds chirruping as they hopped from bush to bush.

If, at that very moment, Joe had happened to look upwards, he would have seen an extraordinary sight. For right there, flying over the chimney stacks of the house, up, up and away, were two large Canada geese and one seagull. Riding on the back of each goose was a little girl, and riding on the back of the sea gull was a small pixie-like fellow with a cheeky grin on his face.

But Joe missed that. He was heading indoors to see if the two little cousins were there with Clare. He looked around. Then he called out: 'Clare! Clare! Have you got the children upstairs with you?'

He heard her shout down, 'No? I thought they were with you, Joe!'

Joe's heart gave a little thud. He went back outside and started calling Bella and Ellie. He knew all the hiding places because he had played hide and seek with Harry and Ellie a hundred times. He skirted round the herbaceous border and shrubbery. He looked in the hen house, the summer house and all their favourite hiding places. He called and called but there was no response, no movement, not even a snap of a twig.

'Clare! Clare!' he shouted urgently. Clare came down to the garden through the French doors.

Together they started re searching the garden all the places they could think of. They were beginning to get a bit frantic and started running everywhere.

Suddenly Joe heard Clare give a shout from the bottom of the garden. 'OH NO! Quick! Come here! Look at this, Joe!'

And there, pinned to the tree was the note that Ellie and Bella had written.

Chapter 27

Riding on the top of the two Canada geese Alberta and Nova was a truly amazing experience for the two little cousins Bella and Ellie. The steady, slow, rhythmic beating of the geese's wings and the gentle warmth of their soft feathers lulled the two children so that they felt as if they were in a dream. Everything was so restful; the birds' flying was so level and steady.

As they flew through the blue sky, they looked around them at the wispy white clouds that floated past. Far below them they could see the patchwork green fields covered with groups of tiny grazing cows, chimney stacks on the tops of little houses, villages with church spires and little roads with small moving cars on them. A couple of doves flew alongside the geese for a little while. 'Ooh noo,' they warbled, as pigeons do.

The girls were interested to see that Alberta and Nova seemed to take it in turns to be at the front. Each bird would fly slightly above and in front of the other bird.

'Why are you doing that?' called Bella to Alberta.

The goose honked back in her funny nasal voice, explaining that they take turns being in the front, falling back when they want a rest.

'There's more wind at the front which is more tiring,' honked Nova, 'If you are at the front you take the brunt of the breeze,' adding 'and we can see better flying in formation like this. It's what we always do. Sometimes when there are lots of us it's really important to fly in a V shape. In that way, we can fly for hours and hours before we must stop for rest. Also, we like to flap our wings and then glide for a bit, just like this!' And as the two birds stopped beating their wings, immediately everything became smooth and silent as they glided through the sky.

The two children were delighted. 'Wow that feels so lovely!' laughed Ellie.

Above them a white seagull swooped into view and flew alongside 'Halloo!' called Magic Joe – he looked just like a little horse-racing jockey. 'How are you all getting on?'

'We're all fine, Magic Joe!' they honked and called together.

'We'll be flying over Kettleburgh in a minute. Look out for your house Bella! What we are looking out for is a large cardboard box in your garden.'

Tom and Dee Dee's house came into view.

'Look there it is!' cried Bella, 'I can see Daddy's car and look — there's our swing in the tree!'

The two geese and the seagull gracefully circled around over the top of the house. The garden looked peaceful in the afternoon sunlight, the fields beyond, fresh golden and green on that early summer's day.

Everybody peered below them.

Suddenly, there was an almighty whoosh! A big brown cardboard box flew past them at incredible speed.

Inside the box you could hear muffled shouts of 'Oh look! It's Bella and Ellie... and who's that? What the... ?!'

Ellie and Bella gave a scream, it was so thrilling!

'Ah... right on cue!' grinned Magic Joe.

'Excuse me!' came a grating squawking from Ray the seagull, 'I don't want to be a nuisance, but I'd quite like to land and rest my wings for a minute.' Ray was exhausted by circling round and round the garden and also thought that maybe, just maybe, there might be the odd potato chip somewhere to eat.

'Oh! So sorry, Ray! Of course you must rest! Let's land in the field just near the gate there at the back of the house. Let's go out of sight behind that oak tree. It will be good to have a chat with the others and see if they have found Ogo Pogo.'

Once again, he drew the little wooden carved stick out of his shoulder bag. 'I think it's time for a little intervention,' he muttered. Circling the stick round in each direction three times he called out:

'*Box! Box! Land with ease.*
Go and hide behind those trees.'

And sure enough, the box landed neatly behind a huge oak tree on the edge of the garden.

Ray landed Magic Joe just next to the box at exactly the same moment. Alberta and Nova did beautiful graceful landings behind them all. Magic Joe dashed helter skelter into the box.

'Shhhh!' he whispered... 'Be very quiet. Bella, Ellie, quickly, come in here and join us.'

With that Bella and Ellie slid down the soft feathers of the two geese. They both gave the geese enormous hugs and kisses and whispered, 'Thank you! Thank you!' in their ears and left them grazing on the grass behind the tree. The girls crawled quietly into the box. It looked so homely somehow with padded lifejackets to sit on. Everyone sat in a circle.

Bea gave Bella the biggest of hugs. She was SO glad to see her... 'Wow, Bella! Was that a goose you were actually riding on? That's so cool. I've been so worried about you!' she whispered.

'That goose is my friend,' said Bella. 'Her name is Alberta.'

'My goosey friend is called Nova,' announced Ellie. 'She is a magic goose!'

Harry gave Ellie a big cuddle, 'Well done Ellie!' he said. 'We went to Nacton and found your note on the tree. We all decided to come straight here!'

Alex looked at Magic Joe... 'So YOU'RE Magic Joe!' Alex smiled. Gosh am I glad to see YOU! My watch has been going berserk all morning. It keeps whirring and winding itself backwards and the date has changed to yesterday. Perhaps you might be able to magic it better?'

'Well, first things first. May I say, I am absolutely delighted to make your acquaintance children,' said Magic Joe with a huge grin. 'Alex, don't worry, your watch is just letting you know that you have travelled back in time again. You are now back to yesterday at around an hour after you left this house. I hope you are all feeling quite well? And, may I ask, did you manage to find Ogo Pogo?'

'How do you do, Magic Joe, we've heard so much about you. Yes, he's right here,' replied Sophia. And she gently opened her pocket. Peering in, Magic Joe could see that Ogo Pogo was lying there curled up looking weak and breathing heavily.

'But oh dear!' said Sophia, 'I've been worrying about him all morning – he just doesn't seem right.'

'Oh, well done for finding him, children! It can't have been easy and everyone will be so proud of you. But no, I'm afraid he wouldn't be feeling too good, actually,' replied Magic Joe. 'You see, we need to get him back to be with his brother Ege Pege as soon as possible. He absolutely HAS to be with him soon and get some rest and recuperation in the matchbox, or he will surely get dangerously ill. He's simply fading away and all the magic in the world will not revive him until he is home.'

The children gasped and Sophia went a little pale.

'Come on!' she cried, 'What are we waiting for? Let's go, right now.'

Ellie looked anxious 'But, we left a note for my Mummy and Daddy saying we had gone to Tom's house and if they come and look for us here, they won't find us, will they?'

'True fact, Ellie,' said Alex.

'I think, Ellie, that you could write another little note for them to say we have ALL gone to Rose's house. And that will do for Tom and Dee Dee as well. In a little while, judging by the time, Dee Dee will be back from the shops on her bike, to make the cake. I don't exactly know where Tom is but... Oh dear!' Magic Joe stopped whispering abruptly.

From across the garden came the sight and smell of bonfire smoke. Peering from the side of the box they could all clearly see Tom with a pitchfork lifting weeds and old bits of wood onto his garden fire. There was a lot of smoke. He was whistling a tune as he did it.

'Oh! There's Daddy!' said Bea in a whisper... 'And look, here's Mummy coming round the corner with the bag of shopping. What ARE we going to do?'

Chapter 28

Bea and Bella dashed across the garden to Tom.
He was engulfed in bonfire smoke and looked a bit
hot and bothered.

'Ah great, you're back you two! Mission
accomplished?'

'Yes but Daddy, we need to go a bit further.
We found Ogo Pogo and now we just want to finish
the mission and take him back to Parham with the
others. We won't be long, honestly, we simply
MUST go — and soon.'

'Well, that's wonderful news,' replied Tom
'Well done! I'm really proud of you. That is
fantastic!'

He walked away from the fire and sat on the
grass away from the smoke looking at his two
daughters who knelt down next to him. He was so
proud of them. It seemed to him that they
appeared somehow different. They looked a little,
well, a little older perhaps? He could see that
they were bursting to go. He also sensed that it
was best not to make too many inquiries.

'Hmmm.' He considered them and then said,
'But I'm afraid I do think you need to go and tell
your mother you want to go to Parham yourselves.
I'm sure if you explain everything, she won't mind
a bit you completing your adventure.'

'Oh but Daddy, can't you explain? She might
say we can't go,' asked Bea.

Tom thought for a minute. 'No, sorry you two. You need to go and talk to her for yourselves.'

The girls looked absolutely crestfallen. 'OK, Daddy if we really must.' said Bea.

Bea and Bella ran across the garden and into the house by the front door. They made for the kitchen. There was lovely Dee Dee unpacking the shopping. She was laying the butter, lemons, eggs and sugar out on the counter by the sink. She glanced up at the children as they came in and gave them one of her big smiles.

'Hello, you two! Have you been having a happy time? Phew! I can tell you, market day in Framlingham was really busy. I feel like I've been gone for ever. I had to queue up in the Co-op to get everything and then I couldn't find any lemons and had to queue at a market stall. Then the chain came off my bike and I had to fix it. Now I feel in a frantic rush to get this cake made in time for tea.' She looked at her watch. 'Oh gosh, it's one o'clock already! Did Daddy give you some lunch?' And she washed her hands thoroughly and then squatted down and got a big mixing bowl out of the cupboard under the counter. 'Do you want to help me, Bea and Bella?'

This last question was the one that the girls had been dreading. Did they want to help Mummy? No, not really, not right now. But how could they explain?

Bea gulped. 'Well Mummy, er... we have got something REALLY important to do. You see, we have got to go with Magic Joe and the others to put Ogo Pogo back in his matchbox. We really want to go and, although we'd love to help you, we really want to finish this thing off.'

Dee Dee nodded. 'Oh, that's nice, girls.' She was carefully cutting the butter up and dropping it into the mixing bowl. She looked as if she was concentrating and was counting the little cubes she had cut up. 'Sounds like a great game,' she added without looking at them.

'Yes Mummy,' added Bella. 'It's true, we are going in a magic box with ALL the cousins.'

'Uh uh, sounds terrific,' murmured Dee Dee abstractedly. Now she was breaking eggs into the bowl and counting them as she went.

'Yes' said Bea, 'and Bella rode on a flying goose called Alberta.'

'Well, how lovely, that's super,' replied Dee Dee, counting the spoonfuls as she measured the coconut sugar into the bowl. She was concentrating hard. She started blending the butter, sugar and eggs together with a wooden spatula.

'Sounds like you're having a proper adventure you two!' And she started beating the mixture as if her life depended on it. 'You'd better go and finish your game then! I'll be ok here. See you later! Don't forget we're going to Rose's in a little. Have fun!' She started measuring the ground almonds into a cup.

'OK Mummy, see you later!' the two girls chorused.

They dashed out of that kitchen like greased lightning. It was only after they had disappeared out of the kitchen that Dee Dee suddenly looked up with a quizzical expression on her face.

They ran across the garden towards the oak tree. Tom was wreathed in billowing smoke on the other side of the garden.

'Phew!' panted Bella. 'Mummy was awfully understanding, wasn't she Bea?'

'Yes! That's because she thought we were making it all up!' replied Bea, laughing.

They got back to the box and wriggled inside to join the others. They briefly explained what had happened and all the children smiled.

'Bea, we have one more thing for you to do now before we go,' said Magic Joe. 'We need you to go and wedge this note under Tom's windscreen wipers on his car. It's just to tell them and Joe and Clare where we all are.'

Bea glanced at the note, it said:

We hav all gon to Parham. See you there. Love from Harry, Ellie, Bea, Bella, Alex and Sophia x x x x x x.

Bea took a deep breath of air. Crawling out of the box she peered round the oak tree and checked the garden. Smoke was still billowing from the other side of it. She sped past the house to the driveway. Her heart was pounding. She did not want to be seen or stopped! She carefully folded the note and pushed it under the windscreen wiper blade and then miraculously, without event, hared back to the tree and disappeared behind it. Breathing heavily, she wriggled back into the box.

Magic Joe, Bella and Ellie were just finishing stroking the two geese and saying thank you and farewell. They all crawled into the box.

'Right everyone. Ready?' said Magic Joe.

'We play in the box,
We play in the box,
We play in the box,
All day!
Take us to Rose and Jon's house.'

They ALL chorused the magic chant together and the box immediately shot up into the sky. Ray the seagull flapped his wings, took off and elegantly followed it. Alberta and Nova beat their wings, ran up the field, took off and sedately flew away in the opposite direction.

The geese flew away over the fields

Chapter 29

Joe and Clare were in their car driving to Kettleburgh from Nacton as fast as Joe dared go.

'Oh do hurry, Joe, I'm beside myself with worry! Can't you put your foot down? No look, stop the car! I'll drive.'

Joe came to a screeching halt in the nearest layby. Clare dashed round the front of the car and got into the driving seat, while Joe wriggled into the passenger seat. He knew Clare would be less anxious if she was driving.

'Don't worry Clare, they'll be alright. We're nearly there and they'll all be safe and sound, you'll see.'

They pulled into Tom and Dee Dee's driveway and got out of the car. They could smell the bonfire and see Dee Dee in the kitchen by the open back door.

'Hi you two!' said Dee Dee. 'Just putting the cake in the oven — be with you in a minute. Tom's round the back.'

Joe and Clare skirted round the side of the house. They rushed across the garden towards Tom who greeted them warmly.

'Tom, have you seen Ellie and Bella?' asked Clare urgently.

'Er... not exactly,' said Tom. 'I've seen Bella... and Bea... but not Ellie.'

'Oh dear, this is all a dreadful muddle!' cried Clare and started wringing her hands in distress, tears filling her eyes.

Dee Dee walked over to join them. 'What's up?' she asked. 'Where are Harry and Ellie... Haven't you got them with you?'

'NO!' came the chorus from Joe and Clare.

The four adults started searching the garden. They skirted round the boundary of the garden onto the fields. Dee Dee jogged up the field to the rabbit holes, where Bella fed the wild rabbits with carrots and apples . They searched the coal shed, the play house and behind the swings. They searched the house upstairs and downstairs. They even looked in the ride-on shed. There was nothing and no trace of any children.

 But had they been very observant, they would have noticed a few stray Canada Geese feathers lying around the oak tree.

Tom walked around to the drive. He saw something that looked like a parking ticket stuck under his windscreen wipers. 'What's this?' At LAST he had found the children's note on his windscreen.

We hav all gon to Parham. See you there. Love from Harry, Ellie, Bea, Bella, Alex and Sophia × × × × × ×.

'Ah' he said and showed the others. 'Look, let's sit down and have a drink and calm down.'

'I've got a hunch that there is a very simple answer to all this confusion.'

They went back into the house, they sat round the large dining table as Tom poured each of them a glass of sparkling water with ice.

'Now look,' said Tom 'we all know that the children have been on an important mission today to find the missing Ogo Pogo.'

'What?' said Dee Dee. 'I thought that was a made-up game, pure imagination! Are you sure? You mean all that stuff about magic boxes, flying geese and Ogo Pogo was true?!'

'It certainly wasn't made up!' replied Tom, smiling. 'But now, I suggest, we simply HAVE to trust them to finish the job off. We don't know where they have been or what they have been up to, and in many ways, I don't think we should EVER ask them. Or be too inquisitive. It's their childhood adventure and we should just let them tell us whatever they like when, and if, they ever want to.'

'Yes, I agree.' said Joe, 'Magic Joe is with them and I feel pretty confident that he will look after them all. We know that Bella and Bea are both safe as you and Dee Dee talked to them recently. That would imply that Ellie, Harry, Alex and Sophia are safe too. The note tells us that they are all together. I think we must simply keep quiet, trust and allow everything to evolve.'

Clare looked a little relieved and much happier. She agreed that they should keep calm and just continue with the day. 'But let's just get over to Hillcrest as soon as we can!' she added.

The mouth-watering smell of luscious lemon cake permeated the room. Dee Dee looked at her watch and gave a gasp: 'Two o'clock! Time to get the cake out of the oven!'

Chapter 30

The magic box landed right down at the bottom of the field near woods just by Jon and Rose's huge old oak tree. Next to the box landed Ray the seagull nonchalantly. All the children crawled out.

'Phew, here at last,' said Harry straightening himself up. 'Am I glad to have got here safely. I could do with a good run about!'

'Me too!' added Sophia

Alex glanced at his watch; the hands were whirring again. 'Golly, it's going backwards again — it's now saying it's two fifteen. It's properly confusing.'

Magic Joe looked at all the children and beamed. 'This certainly is a lovely wood you've got here, Alex and Sophia. Wow! And look at this beautiful oak tree! He skirted round its huge base, peering at all the nooks and holes, the branches. Hmmm... be a good place to make a home don't you think?'

Bella and Ellie looked at each other and gave a little nod.

'Well, we've been thinking that you and Merry should move to this wood — or look, there's another one over there!' said Bella pointing to the plantation on the other side of the field. 'You'd be better living near where to Ogo and Ege live, so you could keep an eye on them, and you could ask Merry to come and live here too.'

'And we could come and see you,' added Ellie, 'as none of us live too far away.'

'Yes, I would absolutely love that!' said Sophia.

'Me too!' said Harry.

'And we could all build you a tree house with my tools,' added Alex suddenly feeling excited and inspired. In his mind he could already see a wonderful little tree house full of gadgets and useful pulleys and bungees.

Bea said, 'Oh Alex! That would be brilliant! Merry has the most amazing little tree house and I could draw it for you to copy!'

'Right well, it's certainly an idea and a wonderful offer! Thank you all of you, that's very kind indeed! I will talk to Merry and we will definitely think about it!' and Magic Joe gave them a wink with a big grin. 'But first things first, we need to get little Ogo Pogo back into his matchbox. He needs some healing, and Ege too, and then, well, Ray and I will be off back to see Merry.'

'Oh, but please don't go, Magic Joe,' said Ellie. 'We love you. Can't you stay for tea?'

'Oh no! Thanks all the same,' said Magic Joe. 'I don't want to sound rude, but I absolutely hate parties and I'm not too keen on grown-ups either. They are SO noisy and bossy with their big booming voices. Besides which, I very rarely show myself to the grown-ups unless there is a dire emergency.'

'Now then, Sophia,' said Magic Joe with some urgency, 'please can you run as fast as you can and go and collect the match box with Ege in it, from the house. Harry please would you go with her as far as the hedge to the house by the garage and keep a look out. I want to know if you see any cars arriving, any grownups. But don't get caught! You shouldn't be here yet, not until the other grown-ups arrive. I don't want Rose or Jon to see you. OK? Sophia before you go, please could you gently lay Ogo on this little tree stump. The others and I will look after him until you get back.'

Sophia very carefully pulled little Ogo out of her pocket. He was curled up and looked very small and very pale. He was still breathing heavily. His eyes were shut. She lay him gently on the tree stump.

'Now hurry! And don't get stopped by anything at all!' said Magic Joe.

From his shoulder bag he pulled his little wooden wand. He circled it three times in each direction and said:

'Run! Run! Through the trees,
So fast, so quiet, no one sees!'

With that, Sophia and Harry set off, sprinting uphill up the side of the woods on the path next to the lane. At the top they turned right and circuited round the field behind the hedge to the garage. Sophia felt she had never run so fast in all her life. Even at her running club she had never run so quickly. In fact, she imagined she could run for ever. She felt like Dash the superhero from 'The Incredibles'. She wondered if her feet were actually touching the ground and she didn't feel the least bit out of breath.

Harry had a huge smile on his face, 'I'm Usain Bolt. I'm about to beat my 100 metres world record of 9.58 seconds.' He giggled to himself he felt SO happy. He LOVED it. The two children ran so fast they didn't seem to take any time at all to reach their destination.

'Heavens above! Look at them go! They look like rockets! Go, Soph and Harry! Go!' called Alex.

Harry and Sophia stopped short just behind the fence to the garage. They squatted down and peered round the corner. They could hear the sound of hammering somewhere near the compost heaps beyond the perimeter of the garden to the left. 'That'll be Daddy,' whispered Sophia. They could hear talking.

Rose was saying '...but Jon, we do need to turn the compost quite soon, shall we do that later this evening after everyone's gone home? By the way, where ARE the children? You did give them lunch, didn't you? I suppose they're down the field somewhere?'

'Well, I haven't seen them for a quite a bit,' said Jon in his matter-of-fact voice. 'I did put some lunch out for them in the kitchen, tried to call, but I think they're down at the pond playing and honestly... Well, I've just been SO busy. I figured they'd come when they're hungry and...' his voice trailed off.

Sophia didn't hesitate. She bolted up the path, through the little side gate and into the side door to the boot room. She dashed through the kitchen and up the stairs to Alex's room. Gently she picked up the matchbox off the window sill. 'It's ok, Ege,' she whispered quietly, 'we've found Ogo!' Popping the matchbox into her pocket, she bolted down the stairs again. Her heart was thumping as she dashed through the kitchen. 'I mustn't bump into Mummy! I mustn't bump into Mummy!' she said to herself.

She was out of the door like a dart. She moved like lightning. Skirting round through the gates back to the fence by the garage she found Harry.

'Look!' he cried. Zooming up the drive were two cars... one with Tom and Dee Dee in it, and the other containing Joe and Clare.

Oh my God!' whispered Sophia urgently. 'Harry! QUICK! RUN!'

Chapter 31

Kind Magic Joe gently lay Ogo Pogo next to Ege Pege in the match box. Ege Pege gave him a long hug and with tears in his eyes squeaked in his tiny broken voice, 'My dear brother, I am so relieved to see you! I've been worried sick and I have felt lost without you.' Looking up at all the children he added, 'I can't thank all of you enough!' and he started weeping again.

Ogo Pogo gave a little sigh and opened one eye, 'I'm so sorry,' he croaked, only to close it again.

Magic Joe carefully slid the match box shut and laid it back on the nearby tree stump.

'Hold hands, children, and make a circle around the tree stump.' The six children held hands, 'put your right hand up and your left hand down, like this.' And Magic Joe showed them how to receive and give in a circle holding hands. The rays of afternoon sunlight fell on the circle of small children. Dust motes danced in the sunbeams around them. They looked like tiny fairies. A bee buzzed around nearby. Magic Joe stood in the middle, lightly touched each of the children on their shoulder with the wand and then, laying the wand's tip on the match box, started repeating quietly:

'Mother Nature of all life,
Fill this woodland place with light.
Share your beauty and radiant love,
With all that live below and above.

Please take away all creatures' pain,
Restore their health and happiness again.
The time has come, renewed by sun,
To count our blessings one by one.'

The children began to feel a little glow passing round the circle from hand to hand. They could feel a tingling sensation. As it increased, they felt warm and content inside. If any of them were tired or thirsty or hungry, they didn't feel it anymore. They began to feel alive and well. There was a sense of belonging to this beautiful wooded place in nature, so settled, close to the trees, in the sunlight. The sound of the birds twittering and the wind in the leaves filled their senses alongside the lovely smell of grasses and the fragrant flowers. They had a real feeling of confidence and pride in their achievement. Connected and close to each other, the cousins could feel their related ancient ancestral blood line running through each of them, bringing them together in harmony. They could feel the presence of their little lost brother and cousin, Sammy, as he sat peacefully on the knee of Grandpa Anthony in Heaven.

And their sixth sense told them that everything would be alright. That all would be well.

As they each opened their eyes, they saw Tinkerbell the cat had quietly joined them and was sitting as still as a statue, nearby, watching them all with her wise green eyes. Ray the seagull was resting in the sunlight, his eyes closed. He looked so regal, and suddenly so beautiful.

Chapter 32

So that's the end of the adventure... nearly...
There's not much more to tell.

The six cousins carried the lifejackets, the old borrowed jackets, smelly old caps and binoculars up to the house and left them behind Tom's car. They put the rope behind Joe's car.

Harry put Jos's torch in the utility room to give back to Gar Gar; she and Jos would be coming over shortly. Gar Gar would read her grandchildren a bedtime story.

The adults were in the dining room drinking tea; Dee Dee was cutting up the cake. She smiled broadly at the children as they all clattered in.

'Well, here you all are at last,' said Rose cheerfully, looking up at the cousins. 'You must be very hungry, I'm sure!' Rose looked radiant and happy. There she was, serene, at the centre of her loving family, hosting a tea party, sitting at her father Anthony's splendid, polished wooden dining room table. In her element. She looked at the children. There was something slightly but perceptively different about them. She couldn't put her finger on it. It was as if they had 'been through' something and seemed a little wiser and older for it.

Alex walked round the table and stood next to Tom. While the others were chattering away. He quietly asked him if he would be kind enough to take the things back to the yacht club back and put them in their rightful places. He also told him that the rib was on the wrong mooring. Tom didn't flicker an eye lid, didn't ask any questions, but simply gave Alex a long gentle hug and said, 'Don't worry, old chap, I'll sort it out tomorrow with Jon.' Sophia came over and clambered up onto Tom's knee and leant herself into him contentedly.

Bea and Alex took the pen knife over to Joe. Joe gave Bea a kiss and put her on his knee. He didn't ask any questions; he just stroked her hair and she felt safe and happy. 'It's OK, Alex,' Joe said, you keep that pen knife — I'm sure you can find more of a use for it than me, and I know you'll give it a good old clean up with some steel wire and some oil.'

Alex was so grateful. 'Thanks Uncle Joe!' And he whispered in Joe's ear... 'We found Ogo Pogo by the way... We followed the clues.'

'Ah that's SO great!' whispered Joe. 'I'll tell the others; they will be relieved. We are SO proud of you all, by the way.'

But no more was said.

Ellie clambered up onto Clare's knee and cuddled into her, with her thumb in her mouth sleepily.

Bella climbed up onto Rose's lap and twiddled with Rose's hair, trying to plait it like a pony's.

Harry and Alex eyed up the wonderful spread of food hungrily, plonked themselves on chairs either side of Jon and grinned at him. He patted their heads affectionately. Everyone settled down for the long-anticipated tea party.

Ray, with Magic Joe on his back, flew to the window ledge of Alex's room. The window was still open. As the sun began to go down behind the trees, in the golden light, Magic Joe carefully placed the match box safely on the inside of the window in the room on the sill. He patted it gently and said, 'Goodbye, Ogo and Ege. Take care of yourselves. See you again one day.'

Ray and Magic Joe were soon nearly out of sight, Ray's beating wings way above the trees heading towards the coast, with Magic Joe riding like a little jockey on his back.

And as for the magic box? Well, later that evening, Alex and Sophia lugged it up the field and over to the trampoline near the house where they played with it, jumping up and down in it until dark. But somehow they didn't feel like chanting the magic spell again.

And that night it rained so hard that by the morning the box had become a mass of soaking, slimy cardboard mush.